Storm Curry is the author of *Winners*. She wrote this book during the pandemic to allow readers an opportunity to enter into a world of fantastic excess, never before seen beauty, luxury and our wildest dreams and fantasy life styles. *Winners* is Storm Curry's literary gift to all day dreamers and visionaries.

This book is dedicated to everyone who never gives up.

Storm G. Curry

WINNERS

AUSTIN MACAULEY PUBLISHERS™
LONDON • CAMBRIDGE • NEW YORK • SHARJAH

Ordering Information
Quantity sales: Special discounts are available on quantity purchases by corporations, associations, and others. For details, contact the publisher at the address below.

Publisher's Cataloging-in-Publication data
Curry, Storm G.
Winners

ISBN 9798886931419 (Paperback)
ISBN 9798886931426 (ePub e-book)

Library of Congress Control Number: 2023921378

www.austinmacauley.com/us

First Published 2024
Austin Macauley Publishers LLC
40 Wall Street, 33rd Floor, Suite 3302
New York, NY 10005
USA

mail-usa@austinmacauley.com
+1 (646) 5125767

A word of acknowledgment from a grateful author. I would like to thank my family for allowing me the space to create these characters during one of the most horrific times in our lives. Thank you, Madison, Clarke, and, of course, thank you, Bobby.

StCyR Peters

Imagine a man so handsome he could easily be mistaken for a woman. Other men view him as a threat, not only to their manhood, but they would rather not have him around their women. Then there are those who automatically think, "Yeah, he's gay."

"Of course, he's gay," some would say, with no evidence or proof of such. "No straight guy looks like that. He's either gay or confused about his sexuality," is how a former coworker describes him. Straight men, gay men, and straight women presume he's a player. Behind his back, the whispers were of his many conquests, but his reality would read differently.

When describing StCyR's outward appearance, one would think you're receiving the physical qualities of a woman. He's tall with skin the color of sand, hair the color of sand, and eyes that are rich with a mix of caramel and sunlight. His eyes produce a sunburst within them, dead center. If that weren't enough, he has a slim build and a muscular frame. His movements are very catlike and rhythmic.

Be that as it may, StCyR Peters is a living, breathing contradiction. His very limited experience with women and romance is unknown to the world, and that suits him just fine.

People are instantly attracted to him because he exudes warmth, but the one thing that always attracts both women and men is his infectious smile. That smile is often mistaken for interest, and the person on the receiving end of it is often left, well, puzzled. His lack of follow up has left many confused, while others frustrated, even angry.

StCyR is also very knowledgeable, but his attention span is lacking. He could have easily finished college, but his interests were so varied, he couldn't complete one task before starting another. He would spend days in the university library, buried in books regarding world religions, politics, art, anthropology, physics. He was attracted to many different pursuits, which did not allow him to choose a single pathway of study. There was always something more interesting than the last. The magnetic pull of the next subject matter kept StCyR passionate about life and curious about the unknown. It also kept him from earning a degree. His love of learning new things was a gift/curse from his mother, whom he adored.

His mother was only 16 years older than him, so she was more like a sister and a friend.

StCyR's mother left home when she was 16 years old. Random StCyR was born and raised in Crescent City, New Orleans. Random was the eldest daughter of her family. Random, though a mere child herself, was a second mother to her five siblings. Every morning, she packed school lunches, made breakfast and helped dress them for the day. This routine would begin when Random was barely five years old and continued throughout her young years.

Raising her mother's children was not Random's choosing, yet it became her obligation, and ultimately, her destiny.

At age 16, Random found herself pregnant and living with an older man. After abandoning her siblings to have a quieter, simpler life, there she was, pregnant herself. "At least she was with a man she loves, and she would take care of her own baby." The irony of still raising a child was not lost to her, as she was deeply in love with her unborn child and the father.

The thought of this life was so dreamy and rich that Random didn't care what anyone thought of her union with Milan.

The unlikely pair met when Random worked after school at a boutique in The Quarter. Random loved her job at her favorite boutique as it gave her an escape from home life and allowed her creativity to flow. The shop owner was impressed with Random's ability to dress the boutique window with a flair that kept the patrons stopping in and shopping like it's an Olympic sport.

One day, Random decided to turn the display window into a live one. She and the other store clerks dressed themselves in the boutique's latest fashions, and Random strategically placed the ladies in the store window. The result was breathtaking. The customer flow was incredible, and at the end of the shift, the boutique owner raved about Random's successful idea. Just as the shop was about to close, Milan Whittaker walked in. He locked eyes with Random—and the rest, as they say, "is history." Unbeknownst to Random, Milan walked by that window at least 20 times throughout the day. He had to build up his courage to approach her. Never in his life did he feel the need to have someone become a part of his existence. The feeling was so overwhelming that it brought on a sudden surge of anxiety. He tried walking away and forgetting he had ever seen her, but something about her would not allow him to leave. After spending most of the day staring at her from across the street and passing the window several times for a closer look, Milan knew he had to take a chance.

Milan and Random were inseparable. Milan moved her into his space where they would build their lives together. Random felt euphoric when Milan was around, and her heart ached when he wasn't in her presence. What Random didn't know is that the man she fell instantly in love with is also married to a prominent local socialite, and the apartment she shares with Milan belongs to his wife's family. Milan Whittaker is having his cake and eating it too. He has his own family and lives a double life with Random.

One day, while riding the streetcar from a visit with her friends at the boutique, Random spots Milan's distinctive car, parked in the shopping center along Carrollton Avenue. She's excited and immediately pulls the car string to get off at the next stop. Random exits at the next stop and begins the slow trek in the direction of Milan's car. There were several adorable little shops along the way. Uptown New Orleans was known for its eccentric mix of exclusive party supply stores, heavenly smelling candles and scents' shops, Boudoir specialty stores, and bakery kitchens. The chocolatier there is otherworldly, and no one leaves the square without making a new friend and ordering a cocktail to go. The ice cream parlor only sells ice cream infused with bourbon, gin, and liqueurs from around the world. The very popular tree-lined street, Carrollton Avenue, is mostly known for its established restaurants, and Uptown New Orleans is full of them.

Random could smell the roux percolating as she searched the windows and doors of the shops. This is the place where one talks about their next meal while eating their current one. She looks up at the gallery level, where hanging ferns flourish, and creeping ivy is perfectly woven through the intricate ironwork. Twinkling white lights add an element of beauty and serenity to the picture-perfect structures.

The scene would not be complete without jazzy blues blasting through the speakers of the marketplace. The Uptown New Orleans Marketplace is so boozy and bubbly it will make you smile, and Random was all smiles as she hunted for her "Honey," Milan. The very thought of him made her smile.

Both her hunt and her smile were short-lived when Random spotted him. She stepped quickly in his direction when, out of nowhere, a young boy, maybe three years old, ran and leaped into Milan's arms. Startled by Milan's ready acceptance of the little boy, Random stopped dead in her tracks. Not knowing what else to do, she slowly pulled back and ducked behind an ornate pillar. Random watched as a woman carrying an infant also entered Milan's space. The woman embraced Milan with a long, loving kiss that could not be mistaken for anything but love. Random felt the room spin a little but managed to contain her emotions. She could feel herself welling up but forced back the tears. In a moment of clarity, she pulled herself together and approached the couple and the children. She walked directly up to Milan with every bit of grace she could muster *up*.

"I'm so sorry," she says. "You look just like someone I used to know," she continued, and abruptly left with tears streaming down her face.

Random was so grief-stricken, she couldn't figure out which way she was going.

Instead of getting back on the streetcar, she hailed a taxicab that took her back to their apartment. The life she once knew had come to an unexpected ending.

Later the same day, Random said goodbye to the apartment she and Milan shared. Before leaving, she left a letter…

My dearest Milan

The saying that all good things must come to an end is so true.

I want you to know that I believed in you and believed everything you ever said to me. There's a lot to be said for the naive.

Anyway, I wish you and your family the best. Please don't worry about us. We will be fine.

BTW, I could have caused a big teenage girl scene and outed you in front of your family, but in spite of it all, I love you too much to hurt you in that way. You have your family, and I know how important family is.

Goodbye Milan
R.—

Random locked the apartment, taking with her the memories of a love affair that broke both her heart and her spirit. She clutched her black velvet jewelry bag—full of the trinkets Milan bought for her. She also packed Milan's Cartier watch and monogrammed money clip. The two thousand dollars in the clip will certainly come in handy to a heartbroken, pregnant, single young girl.

Three months after the breakup, StCyR Milan Peters was born. StCyR was the apple of his mother's eye. She took him everywhere, including work. Random wasted no time finding work, even before StCyR was born. During the last three months of her pregnancy, Random lived with her new employer.

After recovering from the heartbreak of Milan's infidelities, Random began applying for jobs to ensure a future for her and her baby. Scouring the ads for potential gigs was scarier than she wanted to admit. Realistically speaking, who would hire an underaged, pregnant girl? With limited time to gain employment and without showing her hand, or stomach, Random put a plan into motion. She purchased a full-length Red Riding Hood cloak, pulled her sandy colored hair back into a sleek ponytail and poured on the makeup. After all, makeup helps you look older—or so she thought.

A full face of makeup with red lipstick gave Random the appearance of an older person. Instead of looking fourteen, she looked more like 15 and a half. She was barely in her second trimester, so her baby bump was not very revealing. She hardly gained any weight, so concealing her secret under her new red coat was pretty easy.

Random entered the beautiful sitting area at the Gentleman's Club, armed with bravado and the lies she would tell. The club owner turned out to be a woman, which caught Random completely off guard. A man would be easier to persuade and fool into believing she could bump and grind with the best of them. There was no turning back now, so Random mustered up her courage and forged on. "What's the worst that could happen?" she thought to herself.

At first glance, Random thought the woman was laughing at her. Well, she was. The woman stepped forward to Random to do a quick assessment of her, and she laughed again. This time, the woman laughs out loud.

Random was both annoyed and embarrassed. "I don't see anything funny," she snapped and turned to leave. This made the Club Owner laugh even more so.

Random's face was stinging, and she could feel herself beginning to cry. Her hormones were certainly wearing on her now, making it next to impossible to contain herself. Crying was for the weak, and she prided herself on being tough and not leaning on anyone. After all, she left home and never looked back. Random's mother was fine with being fruitful and multiplying, producing one baby after another each year, but Random refused to settle for an ordinary and trivial life. Pregnant or not, she would make a great life for herself and her baby.

But first, Random decided she will confront this rude person, laughing in her face. She turned back to the Club Owner and just when she was about to let her have it, the woman spoke, "I'm so sorry. It's just so funny that most of the girls that apply to work here come dressed in little to nothing. You show up dressed like Sherlock Holmes. Are you nude under that big coat?"

Random began to slowly crack up herself as she now realized why the club owner was so tickled by her. The two of them were suddenly laughing so hard that they were both crying and slapping each other like old friends. As soon as one stopped laughing and looked at the other, they broke into another round of uncontrollable laughter. The Club Owner nudged Random toward her office and invited her to a beautiful box of tissues.

Once they were both sure they could speak without laughing, the Club Owner studies Random as she pulls herself together.

Random began to notice the walls of the club owner's office. They were covered with pictures of some of the most beautiful women she had ever seen. Random suddenly became unglued and cried. As Random wept openly, the club owner sat in silence and carefully examined the specimen before her. There sat Random, a rare beauty with a presence that commanded attention. It was obvious this young girl was self-conscious about her looks and didn't use them to get what she wanted. All of that would soon change.

The woman asked Random to stand and do a twirl around. Random did a slow, sorry spin in her big coat and slick ponytail. The over-done makeup was now streaming down Random's face. Her vulnerability endeared her even more with the Club Owner.

"Take off your coat," the woman said. Random lowers her eyes, then slowly unbuttons her cloak. She realized she could no longer conceal the one thing that would keep her from landing this gig she so desperately wanted and desperately needed. Random slowly peels off her armor and waits for the club owner's reaction. Her heavy cloak was at her feet, and there was nothing standing between the woman and Random's small baby bump.

The club owner begins a head-to-toe assessment of Random's frame and stops at the little protruding belly. After a few ticks, she lets out a knowing, "Aha, I see!" Random cannot move. She stands in front of the club owner and waits for the rejection. The reality of her life was never more evident.

The Club Owner asks, "When are you due?"

"Um, um, June, June 11th," Random stutters. The woman reaches for her calendar, then marks out some details on it. "Okay, you should be ready to work the week of July 20th."

Curious, Random asks, "So, you're hiring me?"

"You want to dance, don't you?" the club owner replies.

"Yes, of course, I just, I just." Random couldn't find the words to express her gratitude.

"Let me tell you something. I found myself in a similar situation some years ago," the woman began. She then went on to tell Random how she was a young girl with no hope, no money, and nowhere to go. As the woman spoke of her experiences, Random began to notice how very attractive the club owner is. She notes her beautiful porcelain skin, dark piercing eyes, lashes for days, and long silky black hair. Her teeth are perfectly straight and as white as snow. "Cosmetic," Random thought to herself.

Random continues to check out her new employer and notices the woman has tattooed rings around her pinky and ring fingers. Random dared not ask the meaning of the tattoos but noted them just the same.

The ladies talked for almost an hour when the club owner learned that Random did not have a permanent home. That information prompted her to lead Random to a door at the back of the club. Random was shocked to learn that the club owner was some sort of "dorm mom" to the ladies that worked the club. There was a Barbie Room that was used to house the expectant mothers and their newborns. There was also a beautiful loft, heavily decorated and charming. The loft was all done up in crisp white fabrics with ivory beige accents. The room smells of jasmine and cinnamon. There were scented candles everywhere and furry throws on the bed and sofas. The room was well lit, with a circular chandelier above the bed that was both massive and spectacular. A beautiful crib sat nestled next to the bed. The crib had matching fabrics like the bed and inside the crib stood a baby giraffe, all decked out in white. Random would call this new place home for the next few months.

On June 11, just like clockwork, StCyR Milan Peters was born. StCyR became the club baby, going from arm to arm. With so many women fussing over him, StCyR could have easily become spoiled, but he was such a good-natured baby. He loved and welcomed all of the attention. The ladies were rewarded with a bond that came so sweetly and naturally from this child. He exuded warmth and responded so positively to everyone around him.

StCyr cast his spell amongst the ladies very early in life. He spent every waking moment looking deeply into the eyes of those around him.

On StCyR's 14th birthday, Random left the club for a new life. Her days of dancing for her very life were finally over. She would be forever grateful for the opportunity to regain control of her life, but just the same, Random and StCyR had a whole lot of livin' to do outside of the club life.

Random and StCyR spent hours online, mapping out the tours they would take, searching for the perfect hotel and seeking out the best restaurants. They didn't want to be traditional tourists; they wanted to see Paris through the eyes of the locals. This trip would be particularly exceptional as both Random and StCyR were curious about their family heritage.

Random's family name on her mother's side of the family is StCyR, the name she gave her only son in honor of her mother's family. Peters is Random's father's last name, but it didn't matter. She and her father have a non-relationship. Random surmised a long time ago that her father had no use for children when they were no longer babies. From time to time, Random's family would cross her mind, but her thoughts never included her father. She couldn't recall a single incident where he acknowledged her, other than to tell her to take care of her younger brothers and sisters, while he ravaged their mother.

Her siblings looked to her for protection, for love, for guidance and camaraderie. Random was conflicted as she had to step into the role of being in charge. She had no support system, and she was a child herself. Here she was, in her teen years, caring for these children, as if they were her own. Both parents were still in the home yet absent from their responsibilities as mom and dad.

It was a very bizarre existence. She no longer had friends as her interests had surely changed. She would see her classmates at the mall shopping and having a good time. She, on the other hand, would be shopping for the children and racing home to get dinner started, do laundry or other mundane tasks.

All her memories involved her thoughts of innocence lost. She didn't have the opportunity to complete her adolescent years.

So, when it comes to her father, no love is lost there. She felt a little sorry for her mother, but not much.

Random and StCyR awakened hours before their scheduled flight. There was so much excitement in the air. They took the streetcar down to the end of the line, where they would purchase their last-minute toiletries from the drugstore. As they exited the drug store, they simultaneously yelled "snacks!" suddenly realizing they would need snacks for the long flight. To save time, they agreed to split their time between the Winn Dixie and the Piggly Wiggly store. Random would get the healthy snacks from the Winn Dixie while StCyR picked up the chips, cookies, candy, and gum from the Piggly Wiggly.

"Okay, Maman," StCyR says with a wide grin. "Let's scrutinize our watches." Random belts out a hearty laugh, as StCyR could always make her laugh. "I'll scrutinize you if you're not back at this spot in 20 minutes," Random teases. With that, the two take off running in opposite directions.

Twenty minutes to the second, StCyR lands at the same spot where they started. Ten more minutes went by and Random hadn't returned. Fifteen minutes passed and Random hadn't returned. StCyR was concerned but not panicked. He took his cell from his backpack and dialed her phone, but there was no answer. He called her a second time and still, no answer. StCyR heads toward Winn Dixie and continues calling.

His thoughts were racing, and his heart was pounding wildly as he began searching the store for his mother. "Maman! Maman!" he yells through the store, wide-eyed and panting! He stops for a moment to catch his breath and to calm himself. As he takes longer, more controlled breaths, he spots a small crowd gathering in one of the store aisles. Through heavy tears, StCyR sees paramedics rushing through the store, people moving quickly, and red flashing lights, but more than anything, StCyR sees his world suddenly come to an end. No goodbyes, no hugs, no kisses, no nothing. In an instant, Random was gone.

The ride to the hospital was blurred with chatter, a long, bumpy ride through the streets of New Orleans, a blaring alarm from the paramedics and fire trucks, and an endless stream of tears. When the ambulance arrives at the hospital, the medical staff receives Random's lifeless, still body, and they take off toward two large metal doors. A medic straddles Random's body, wildly pumping up and down on her chest as StCyR watches in horror. He was told to wait outside the heavy metal doors—and so he waits. And he waits and waits. StCyR waited alone in the waiting area for almost six hours.

At one point, StCyR finds himself folded up in a chair inside the waiting room with a death grip on his Piggly Wiggly bag. The backpack that Random had specially ordered for their trip sat beside him. Random's backpack was somehow tucked inside StCyR's backpack. A bystander that witnessed the tragic events made certain the young boy was given his mother's personal belongings. Someone had also left a Coca Cola and some crackers on the table next to StCyR, but he didn't notice them. He sits quietly, wondering if it was all a bad dream. Reality sinks in when his eyes become focused on the heavy metal doors.

StCyR's grief-stricken, frightened face shows it all. All signs of innocence were replaced with a child's will to die with its mother. There he sat, drained of the life of a young boy, facing an uncertain future. Nothing and no one could console him. Random is everything to him, and now, he fears, she may be gone, forever.

StCyR arrived at the Nicholls Centre the very next day. Before long, the Christmas holidays arrive. StCyR realized he either slept or had been sleepwalking through life during his indoctrination at the Nicholls Centre. The facility was dedicated to the City of New Orleans by the Jesuits. It has become one of the most recognized residential facilities, dedicated to providing shelter, education, and guidance to boys without families.

StCyR, without realizing it, spent the last six months in a dreamlike state, detached from life and living inside his head. He could hear echoes of phrases from the people around him, but his life with Random plays on and on in his mind. He would later describe this time as an underwater stage play. He remembers people speaking to and about him as though he were not there. He knew he was alive because his roommate never stopped talking. He could hear his own heartbeat, which was also a good sign. He finds himself eating here and there, which kept him from starving.

The one thing StCyR couldn't do was to feel alive. He could not accept the loss of his mother. The very thought of her no longer being in his life cut him to the core. Whenever he thinks of her, which is every moment of every waking hour of every day, StCyR can feel his heart breaking all over again. Enduring this level of grief alone while trying to adapt to his new surroundings has shattered his spirit and leaves no room for healing.

One day, while entering the courtyard of the Nicholls Centre, StCyR plants his feet firmly onto the pavement and faces the sun. At that very moment, a beautiful, colorful bird flies past his ear, lightly brushing against his hair. StCyR wonders if the bird is a messenger or Random herself. He thought about the bird the rest of the day. He visualizes a playful Random using this life form to visit him.

StCyR has barely uttered a word during his stay at the Nicholls Centre. Suffice it to say, most of the boys there would not recognize him in a lineup, have no idea what he sounds like and will probably have no recollection of his existence in the future. It is dinner time, and most of the young boys stampede the dining room, eager to partake of the day's libations. StCyr could feel his body being pushed along the corridors, knowing he was on a journey to some place, but his thoughts, as usual, weren't clear. Many of his actions during that time were mere reflex motions, done with little or no thought on his part.

On this day, StCyR focused and could see the sights and hear those around him. For the first time since his mother's passing, he could smell the aroma of the truly delicious foods prepared by staff who pride themselves on their dishes. These are no ordinary cafeteria cooks but culinary heroes, putting out the most remarkable meals. The chef and his team of sous chefs and bakers were some of the finest New Orleans has to offer. Landing a gig with the Jesuits is both an honor and a golden ticket into some of the finest restaurants in the city. The Catholic hierarchy is well connected in the city and are known to assist in making introductions for their staff. StCyR could feel his soul stirring as the aroma of the Cajun heavy spices jolted him into his new reality.

His thoughts immediately turned to the days he and his mom would whip up some concoction together. They learned to cook meals from their favorite restaurants in the city. Every Saturday they would dine at a different restaurant to pig out. On Sunday, they would duplicate the meal they shared the previous evening with the help of their great assortment of cookbooks.

StCyR thought of the many menus they "collected" from various restaurants over time. They had built up quite the collection, including such gems as The Cheesecake Factory, Jaegers, Commander's Palace, The Ruby Slipper, Fire and Ice, and who could forget the night they ate at Antoine's?

Returning from his reverie, StCyR gathers himself and readies his palette for some variation of gumbo. The room is filled with an unmistakable roux that is undoubtedly the beginning of a tasty meal. His reentry to the world was made easier, knowing that he could eat his next meal with Random by his side. StCyR devoured the food, which also filled him with the warmth of remembrance.

The years went by quickly, and StCyR prepared to leave the Nicholls Centre immediately following graduation. He was grateful for his time spent there. The school offered him shelter, education, and some of the best food the city could offer. His mind was set on finding his way in life, and his new journey was somewhere in The Crescent City, outside the walls of the Nicholls Centre.

StCyR immediately enrolls at Tulane University, which is a few blocks from the Nicholls Centre. So much for venturing out on his own. Tulane afforded scholarships to the boys of Nicholls to continue their education. StCyR has no real connections to anyone or anything, so attending a university was a good move from his vantage point. He could easily slide into a life of non-existence and learn a little something along the way.

He spends much of his time in the Tulane library and had become an avid reader, exploring and entrenched in every subject matter. His favorite indulgences include English literature, religion, world history, socioeconomics, and art. He has also developed an interest in international law, physics, and, of course, voodoo culture in New Orleans.

StCyr's cravings for information left him mystified and exhausted. Was there such a thing as too much information? He'd heard the term "TMI" but never imagined it to be more than an acronym. His head was crammed with information, but harnessing the information became his next challenge. Not knowing what to do with this overwhelming abundance of information, he decides to leave the university to define who StCyR would become. He considers himself part scholar, part artist, a culinary visionist, but most of all, a decent human being. University life was a bit too confining and way too structured for him. He needed to breathe and realize his intended path.

He used his savings and the money left from the stipend he received from The Nicholls Centre to move to the Warehouse District near downtown. The lofts of downtown New Orleans are known for their immeasurable high ceilings, spiral staircases, exposed brick walls, and dark hardwood floors with mirror finishes. Local artists flock to the area, so the streets were always pumping with activity. StCyR instantly fell in love with this part of the city. For the first time in a long time, he could feel his whole being. His heart, soul, body, and mind felt aligned. The disjointed feeling that haunted him since his mother's death no longer encased him. StCyR begins to feel again, and he thanks his mother for carrying him this far. "I'll take it from here, Maman," he whispers to himself.

StCyR quickly took to his new surroundings and soon lands a gig at one of the local galleries. With his vast knowledge of art history, the gallery personnel and patrons quickly grow very fond of him. To keep himself busy,

StCyR also took a part-time job as a barista at a coffeehouse.

The patrons at both jobs are very fond of StCyR. He has a hard time figuring out why people stare at him, particularly women. Women of all ages would engage him with idle chatter, and he, unassuming and naive, chatted them all up. His sincerity and grace were a welcome quality that drew people in. His kind spirit and calm manner brings unexpected interest to the workplace. Patrons of both businesses are quickly locked into StCyr's engaging personality. His adoring fans didn't know they were being courted by a young man who is mostly preoccupied with his own thoughts and a grief that follows him wherever he goes. The very concept of sharing his life with another never crosses his mind.

Both the gallery owner and coffee house owners always encourage StCyR's good natured spirit. He is very good for business, and business was good all around. When he became aware that the attention seekers wanted more than conversation and coffee, he gave them just enough of his time to keep them interested. Having two jobs gives him an automatic excuse from committing himself. He always stops short of leading anyone on, though. The Jesuits and his mom gave him a healthy respect for others, and he knew in his heart the emotional distance between himself, and others is best for all concerned parties.

On what would be a rare night off from the coffee house, StCyR decides to take the streetcar down to the Quarter. It was a nice night out, and he had nothing to do. He walks down Bourbon Street and ends up at Cafe Du Monde. "How fitting," he thought. "One barista being served up by another." Café Du Monde is known worldwide for its coffee with chicory, and tourists from around the world would flank the restaurant to partake of the best beignets ever.

StCyR soaked up the atmosphere as he downed 3 rounds of beignets and hot coffee. He watched as the horse-drawn carriages went by and scores of tourists walked back and forth. The streets in the Quarter were always filled with excitement. A jazz quartet blasted the night air with brassy zydeco music while StCyR enjoyed the dusty powdered sugar beignets, which covered his shoes, his pants, his shirt, and his face. Every person at Cafe Du Monde left with a healthy dose of powdered sugar on them.

Before long, StCyR was walking back to the streetcar, headed home. He was stuffed and content, and this outing was a much-needed break from the routine. StCyR could see the streetcars lining up to take off, so he hurriedly ducks inside the Rexall to get a bottle of water. The cashier casually asked if he wanted to buy a lottery ticket. Without much thought, StCyR said, "Why not?" With that, he takes his change and his lottery ticket and dashes for the next streetcar.

He arrives home a little past midnight. His building is eerily quiet, which he attributes to the lifestyle of his always party-ready neighbors. There was always a celebration of some sort in New Orleans. It was either the Crawfish Festival, the Po Boy Festival, Jazz Festival, A Second Line, Mardi Gras, The Jazz and Heritage Festival, The Oyster Festival, A Saints Tailgate Party, a Jazz Funeral, Essence, St. Patrick's Day Parade, Halloween Fest, Another Second Line, Christmas in the Oaks, A Parade-Just Because, St. Joseph's Night-Celebrating the Native American Culture,

Daiquiri Fest, and on and on and on. This city would party and celebrate the opening of a can of beans! Any excuse to party, and they always did.

Since it was so very quiet, StCyR would use his time to wash and tidy up his place. This was another rare moment for him. He wasn't necessarily messy, but his world was never hurried or pressing. No one ever drops in on him, so housekeeping is not at the top of his to-do list. Nothing in his life was given top priority. Nothing seemed urgent, pressing, or crucial. Maybe someday, StCyR's life would have true meaning, but for now, his life was a series of circular movements, work, home, work, home, work, home. As StCyR finishes washing the dishes, folding clothes, and sweeping, he collapses into a deep sleep.

The next day was Sunday, and so the routine began. StCyR's coffee maker sent the wonderful scent of Community Coffee his way. He sprang from his bed to begin the day.

Sunday was StCyR and Random's favorite day of the week. They'd sit on the stoop, drink coffee, and eat raisin toast together. With each sip, they would clink mugs and toast the Twenty-First Century.

StCyR worked the second shift on Sundays, so he would fill his morning with music and exercise. Sundays made him feel alive. Before long, it would be time to go to work, where the lives of others became his focus. Everyone knows StCyR at the coffee house. His presence is a necessary fixture for the business. He has a way of making everyone feel special.

As he arrives at work, he is greeted by his fellow coworkers and a few regulars. The first-shift barista is a perky little 16-year-old who has a mad crush on StCyR. On occasion, she would sit at the counter after her regular shift to shoot the breeze. StCyR would give her a little pat on the head like a puppy and bid her adieu. That small gesture alone was enough to make the girl's heart flutter. She believes StCyR is the most handsome man she had ever seen, and by some standards, he was.

At the end of his shift, he dashes off to his apartment—his private sanctuary, his escape room, his gym, his studio, everything. Each day would provide StCyR with another opportunity to be every man he dreams he will someday become. His mother's constant drumbeat to "become the person you want to be" often haunts him. He is always aware of those words. Knowing Random's life struggles and his own, gives StCyR an appreciation for life that many will never know. Random tried to make everyone around her feel valued and loved. StCyr was inspired by his mom to make others feel supported. Knowing 'The Random Peters' and all that she encompassed, gave StCyR a reason to not just survive-but to thrive and live an abundant life.

His home liberates his inner spirit and gives him so much pleasure. There he could read or play his guitar, watch TV, listen to his music, search the internet or just chill. He taught himself to love his own company, so he was constantly looking for ways to occupy his time. Some days he would make elaborate desserts or time himself with the assembly of a new puzzle. He taught himself to play the guitar and had become pretty good at it. StCyR was never bored. In the back of his mind, he knew why he kept so busy.

By occupying himself and not focusing on anything, StCyR Milan Peters could fill his thoughts with anything but the memory of his mother's passing. If Random just happens to cross his mind, the memory of that dreadful day always crept into his space. Reliving the agonizing moments leading up to Random's demise would play out in vivid detail.

StCyr made a conscious point of always thinking of his mother on his terms. Every memory he stored of her, and their lives together were carefully orchestrated thoughts he stitched together. He would not allow himself to be trapped with thoughts that would consume and torture his soul.

StCyR stood to clear some space in the living room. He picks up his jeans from the night before, emptying the pockets of the contents from his stroll to the Quarter. Carefully placing the mound of change on the table, StCyR checks the remaining pockets and discovers the lottery ticket he purchased from Rexall. He tossed the ticket on the table along with his loose change. StCyR was done for the evening. He shuts off the lights and hops into bed.

The next morning, while brushing his teeth, StCyR bops to the music while getting dressed. His daily routine includes listening to Bounce music to get him started, followed by a quick run through of the daily news. The local news programs gave him another source to occupy his thoughts, and he looks forward to hearing the latest. When the news came on, he would turn the music volume down and give his attention to the evil news.

StCyR loves working at the gallery. His job at the galley gives him a chance to dress up, every day. He sports imported, black dress slacks, a white collared shirt, a black jacket, and shiny black loafers. The gallery owner insists that StCyR slick his hair back into a ponytail. It was the slicking back of the ponytail that escalates interest in *"the man that works at the gallery."* Both men and women would often wander into the gallery off the streets to get a better look at StCyR. It certainly isn't bad for business as several works of art have been sold to many people entering the gallery under false pretenses.

StCyR is the male version of his mother—skin the color of sand; hair the color of sand; and caramel-color eyes with sparkling sunbursts around the pupil. StCyR is indeed an asset to the gallery. He is a walking work of art, a masterpiece to some and hopefully somebody's boo-if they play their cards right. StCyR remains clueless. He has no idea of the effect he has on others. This also makes him more appealing.

StCyr's life at the club allowed him to develop his charismatic sophistication. From the time he was born, StCyr was flocked by beautiful women, around the clock. Every dancer held him, cuddled him, coddled him, and adored him. Over time, he learned, even as an infant, that a smile goes a long way. As a toddler, he exuded confidence and excitement as the dancers returned to the dressing rooms each night. He lived happily among the women that supplied him with an overabundance of attendance and affection. As a young boy, StCyr possessed a smoldering intense gaze that stayed with him in life. He was complimentary of his many "Aunties" but always showed respect for them. He was also very protective of them all. His early life required him to be in the presence of beautiful young women which fostered a genuine interest and fascination in the lives of those around him.

At the end of his workday, StCyR stops by the market to pick up a few items before heading home. Once inside, he clicks on the evil news to see what's happening in the world. At the end of the broadcast, the host announces the winning lottery ticket was purchased locally, but so far, the winning ticket holder had not come forward.

StCyR thought that was interesting and picks up his lottery ticket from the table where he left it. He looks at his ticket, then replays the winning numbers from the news broadcast. As he reads the numbers on his ticket out loud, then reads the numbers on the TV screen, he notices the similarities in the numbers. He reruns the part of the broadcast again, this time studying the screen with greater interest. He plays the recording repeatedly. StCyR rewinds the program twenty-seven times before he was certain he was holding the winning ticket in his hand. For the first time in his life, StCyR opens the window to his apartment and yells out loud, "What the Fuckkkkkkkk!!!!!!!"

Jewels Wright

When Jewels entered a room, everyone knew it. Jewels Wright never entered a room without his jewelry blinging, cologne singing, shoes shining, hair laid, but most of all- dressed to kill. More than anything, Jewels' big ole smile entered the room before he did. His gregarious nature won everyone over. Jewels fancied himself a "lifestyle coach." In his words "Whatever in life you choose to have, Jewels could make it happen." Most people assume Jewels deals in stolen goods, and he lets them believe just that. The thought of getting popular goods "hot off the market" made his business much more lucrative. The masses who crave designer gear believe the deals are better if they are dealt from the trunk of a car. The truth of the matter is that Jewels is no thief; he's a hustler and a businessman.

At age 15, Jewels is tasked with going to school, playing baseball, and working nights at the local supermarket. Juggling all three doesn't faze Jewels one bit. He considered it a challenge only he could handle. He prides himself on doing what he does very well, and with style. Jewels is an overachiever who saw every opportunity as an opportunity.

At school, Jewels strives to be the best. He is a very good student and very popular with his peers. He's also a skilled athlete, playing centerfield and first string. At the supermarket, Jewels' shelves "sparkle". It's not enough for him to finish his shift with fully stocked shelves. His shelves are done with such precision that the management was seriously considering making him the floor manager. They had to remind themselves that Jewels is only 15 years old, and that probably won't sit well with the veterans of the store.

Most of the supermarket workers come to work dressed appropriately for their age and for the type of work they perform. Jewels, on the other hand, shows up in black jeans, a body-hugging, long-sleeve black shirt, and his comfortable Slip Ons. Jewels is super chocolatey, which makes his beautiful white teeth stand out even more so. Stocking shelves is a mundane task, requiring lots of effort but little else. Jewels decided he would become the stock clerk "g-o-a-t." Not only were his shelves always super clean, but every single one of his shelves is always aligned to military perfection.

At the end of every shift, Jewels rewards himself with a hot buttered croissant and a cup of cappuccino. At one in the morning, the only place to accommodate this craving is Mona's Donuts. Mona's is known for its tasty donuts, hot buttered croissants and steamy, creamy cappuccino. Jewels believes Mona put her foot in every cup of cappuccino because Mona's brew is so good. As a matter of fact, Jewels was so impressed with Mona's cappuccino that he became the proud owner of his very own cappuccino machine.

Late one night after work, Jewels stops at Mona's to get his treats when the Master Blend truck pulls up. Jewels watches with fascination as the Master Blend team work effortlessly to refill the cappuccino machine and re-stock Mona's impeccable pantry.

After months of watching this exchange, Jewels decides to make some inquiries of the Master Blend delivery guys.

Jewels was surprised to learn that all Master Blend workers are thoroughly trained to not only deliver the products, but they also have to master the art of blending the various cappuccino mixes, dismantle and reassemble the machines, and describe every Master Blend product sold. Jewels was both intrigued and impressed with the professionalism and wisdom of what he perceived as two coffee jockeys. He learns there is solid wisdom and art in every cup of their product.

Jewels slowly befriends the Master Blend guys and begins purchasing his cappuccino supplies from them, wholesale. As it turns out, the Master Blend guys are also allowed to sell the products, and they were more than happy to sell to Jewels. The Master Blend guys really like Jewels and enjoy his company. So much so, they invite him to their company pool party.

It was at the Master Blend Annual Customer Appreciation Pool Party that Jewels would meet the people who introduced him to "the real world." Jewels would never look back. The Master Blend pool party turned out to be the event of the season. Many top-level athletes were in attendance, as well as several local celebrities, models, influencers, hoteliers, restaurant owners, clothing designers, and luxury car dealers.

The Master Blend banners flew high above Hotel Highland, which hosted the private affair. The music was "on," the food was catered and free, but the topper for Jewels was the ability to rub elbows with those who would become his business associates. By the end of the evening, Jewels had collected cards from some of the top people in the retail business. This was no chance meeting. Jewels was personally introduced to luxury wholesalers and manufacturers of fine menswear and women's wear, top shoe designers, jewelers, athletic wear producers, and Jewels' favorite trend, athleisurewear. This crowd was the introduction to his new life.

Jewels was quick to follow up with the leads he received during the Master Blend affair. He re-introduced himself to the players that best fit into his business mode and began trading in "lifestyles." Jewels parlayed one night of hobnobbing into a full business.

Jewels' business was suddenly booming. He quickly became the 'go to' for his discounted designer labels.

By cutting out the middleman and not having to pay for rented space, Jewels was in great demand. The orders were coming in faster than he could deliver them. His contact list grew steadily, and the designers and their reps loaded him up with the latest trends. Jewels represented a boost in sales for his suppliers, so they rewarded him with bigger discounts, which he could pass on to his growing client list. Business was so good that Jewels had to make the decision to quit his job at the grocery store and quit school. Without hesitation, he quit both.

Once the decision was made to pursue the course of selling designer trends, he needed a spot to call his own. He found and rented a space near downtown where he would be close to his suppliers. The space would also give him a spot to meet with vendors and lay his head.

Jewels' success continued for the next three years. Everyone knew him, and everyone knew he had the best merchandise. Jewels had found his passion. He was uniquely happy, and life was good.

Carving out this niche in life gave Jewels the luxury of taking his grandmother to Bingo once a week, every week. Jewels and his grandmother, Beau, were two peas in a pod. Beau adores Jewels and vice versa. Beau was happy for Jewels' success, but she wanted nothing more than to see Jewels get his high school diploma. "Every successful man should have his credentials in order, Jewels," his grandmother would say. "I know Beau," Jewels replied hurriedly. He hated this conversation with his grandmother. It pained him more than she knew. "I'll do it when I get the time," Jewels would say.

Leaving high school was a decision made on the fly. Jewels could stay in school and finish up, but he also wanted to be of help to his family in any way possible. He would not receive a scholarship for academics nor sports and the last thing he wanted was a bunch of student loans. As much as he loved school, he knew he could find financial freedom in other ways.

The final straw for Jewels' decision to leave school had nothing to do with school or scholarships or anything of that nature. The final push for Jewels was an incident as he was leaving work late one night. He had finally saved up enough money to buy his neighbor's jeep truck and was heading home in it. As he pulled into a busy intersection, Jewels happens upon a traumatic traffic accident that alters his life. He left the scene with strong feelings of sadness for the people that died, anger that he could do nothing to help them and anxiety and guilt that it could have been him. A few seconds earlier, and he would have been in that intersection.

From then on Jewels began to lose interest in school, friends, and life in general. He became very protective of Beau and had difficulty concentrating on anything for too long.

Rather than sinking into a complete black hole of depression and hopelessness, Jewels decides to refresh with the hope that he will give Beau the life she deserves, rather than the other way around. He becomes Jewels, the uncomplicated, untouchable, man about town. Work would become his passion. He would find solace in his decision to work through it. Working all hours of the day and night would fill the void in his life.

Tonight, was just like all Sunday nights for Jewels and Beau. Jewels would pull up to his grandmother's house in his oversized Range Rover. He called his Rover-Junior, as he figures it's a black beauty, just like him. Modesty is certainly not wasted on Jewels. As Beau backs out of the house, Jewels leaps into action. He jumps out of his Range and races to the other side to get the door for her. Jewels opens the gate at the front of Beau's house and offers the deepest bow as the queen strolls through. Beau tries not to laugh at this silly gesture but plays along. He then helps to get her seated with the assistance of a custom lift he installed for her. Beau always pretends she's not impressed with the hydraulic stair lift he installed for her, and Jewels pretends that he doesn't know that she's pretending to not be impressed. Beau also must mention how "he didn't have to go out and buy the biggest truck he could find". Jewels just smiles his big ole smile and lovingly fastens her inside. Jewels races around to the driver's side and hands Beau a helmet that he purposefully hid behind the passenger seat. Beau looks on in horror, then pops jewels on the back of his head once she realizes he was giving her the business. Beau adores her Jewels, and he knows it. He loves his grandmother equally, and she is the only girl in Jewels' life. Right now, his heart has no room for anyone else.

Jewels could only commit himself to love a definitive number of people. Offering love to others meant losing control. In his own strange way, he figures the least amount of people he allows himself to love, the less he has to lose in life. Not accepting offers of love and companionship allowed his mind to soar. He would dream of life in a way where he was never hurt by the loss of a loved one. Financial freedom and freedom from heartache kept him moving forward with no strings attached.

It was Beau's influence that taught Jewels the art of fine living. Beau schools Jewels whenever she can. She lives a modest life from a spectator's perspective, but once inside her home, a discerning eye quickly picks up on a woman with sophistication, style, and flair. Beau has a little money, old money, but she is frugal and as "tight as a drum," Jewels would tease. Beau is very giving when it comes to Jewels. She worked hard all her life to have the kind of life she has. To be able to give her only grandchild the life she never had as a child is a bonus for Beau. She had acquired a taste for the finer things in life over time. "Quality is where it's at!" she preaches. Jewels had no trouble getting Beau's meaning about quality living. The top shelf life is right up Jewels' alley.

Beau loves Jewels' zest for life, but she is concerned that he works too much and needs to find someone to love him as much as she does. Although she loves all of the attention she gets from Jewels, she wants more for him. He's a great person and he needs to find a love interest.

Jewels and Beau enter the Bingo Hall, arm in arm. All of Beau's gal pals are there, and they wave to Beau and Jewels as he ushers her to her favorite seat. Beau is a bit of a fixture at the Bingo Hall, as she has won several jackpots over the years. Her winning spree paid for some of her travels, and Jewels was the lucky recipient of many free trips, courtesy of Beau and The Bingo Hall.

At ten o'clock sharp, the Bingo parlor doors swung open. A mass of people come pouring out, and among them was Jewels and Beau. As they approach Jewels' big ole truck, they begin a full round of singing and dancing. They both belt out "B-I-N-G-O, B-I-N-G-O, B-I-N-G-O, and Bingo was his name-Oh!!!" Jewels and his grandmother howl as he helps her into his truck. He continues the Bingo song as he raced around to the driver's side. Jewels jumped into the car, giving Beau the biggest hug. "Beau, you are the luckiest person I know!" he continues. "It's all in the cards," Beau replies, stuffing her winnings inside her cuff. Beau always dressed for the occasion, and tonight, she looks like a million dollars. She had the aura of a winner, so it was fitting that she took home the gold.

"Once again, you win the grand prize!" Jewels said, shaking his head. "So, what's this like, your ninth grand prize win?" Beau sat back in her seat, looking regal and composed. "It is all in the cards. You've got to choose the right cards."

Jewels starts up the Rover as Beau instructs him to turn on her seat warmer and adjust her mirror so she can help him drive.

They were headed toward Beau's house when she suddenly developed a craving for dessert. "Jewels," she started. "Let's go crazy and have some hot fudge cake and ice cream."

"As you wish, madam" and without hesitation, Jewels whips the Rover around into a crazy U-turn that would have sent most people screaming. Beau simply held on to the road bar and took it all in stride. She was used to Jewels' antics and never flinched. This endeared his grandmother to him so much. For the most part, Beau allowed Jewels to be Jewels. Besides, she was headed to the Night Cap for their special dessert. An illegal U turn was not going to get in the way of that.

These two were no strangers to the Night Cap. They would grab late-night snacks from this establishment all the time. Jewels called ahead and ordered two specials for the road. The molten hot fudge cakes with a side of vanilla ice cream would top off their evening for sure.

When Jewels returned to the truck, Beau was fumbling through her winnings to pay for their desserts. "Aw, come on, Beau!" Jewels said, waving off the money. "Take it or I won't eat it," Beau replies. Exasperated, Jewels takes the twenty dollar bill and stuffed it in his pocket. Beau gave Jewels "the look," which told him she was not playing around. Jewels knew that look and started up the truck. "Okay, Tupac, you win." Beau and Jewels laughed all the way to Beau's house.

The two of them ate their desserts together, conspiring to meet again soon. When they were done, Jewels wished his grandmother a good night and made sure she was securely locked inside. He hops inside his truck and heads home. Jewels has also developed a penchant for after dinner liqueurs and craves one to cap off his night. The mini mart at the foot of the lofts where he lives carries an assortment of liqueurs. The Courvoisier VS would be the perfect topper for the evening.

Jewels grabs a couple of cordial bottles and pulls out the twenty-dollar bill his grandmother gave him from his pocket. The clerk hands Jewels some loose bills and change. "You know, my grandmother gave me the twenty from her

Bingo winnings, so in her honor, let me have some lotto tickets with the change." The clerk wishes Jewels a good night and good luck as he heads up to his loft.

Jewels was busy placing orders and delivering them to his many clients. Part of his boutique business includes Jewels personally delivering to his special client base. Mondays are always both exciting and annoying. Jewels' clients will spend their weekends ordering the latest fashions and Jewels starts the week filling those orders. By Monday night, he is completely exhausted.

His day mostly began with a trip to several designers' showrooms and a trip to several shoe suppliers. He would also visit his favorite jewelers and round out his day at the tobacco bar. The tobacco bar was always his last stop, so he could relax and enjoy the company of his friend, Raul. He and Raul would kick back with a freshly rolled fatty while they listened to the soulful sounds of Marvin Gaye. It was such a joy for Jewels to be in the company of Raul and his family. Raul's father and his father began their cigar business in the basement of their home. After years of sacrifice and hard work, Saldana's Cigar Salon was born and had grown to become one of the finest in the city. Jewels admires the family hustle and is surprised at how much he himself enjoys the sweet leaf. A good cigar and good company were the best ways to round out a hard day's work.

Business was good but being the sole proprietor of his emerging little empire was taking its toll on Jewels. Carving out the deals, selecting the right merchandise, picking up the merchandise, and delivering it to his clients, who sometimes lived as much as 500 miles away, was getting to be a bit much. Jewels was truly exhausted from the demands of his clients, but his drive to do better was the thing that kept him going. He was so grateful for the blessings of his good fortune; he dared not complain.

At 8:39 PM, Jewels pulled into his parking space and trotted to his apartment. He was so happy to be home that he grabbed his couch pillows and hugged them with all his might. Knowing how expensive his shoes were and imagining how Beau would yell at him for putting his shoes on the couch, Jewels slowly slipped out of his Thom Browne patent penny loafers. Being tired was no reason to abuse 1800.00 shoes. The same care was taken with his Movado Men's Valor Tungsten Carbide Watch. Jewels slipped it off his wrist while lying completely horizontal on his couch.

He blindly reached for his remote control and his Motorola Razr. Jewels began checking his messages through tired, bleary eyes when he came across a message from Beau.

"Thank you for a wonderful evening," it read. Jewels smiled at the very thought of Beau texting. He sat with Beau for a full week until she got the hang of it. She resisted and struggled with the very thought of texting, but Jewels convinced her that texting would soon be the universal language and she would be the only person on earth who could not speak it. Beau knew he was full of caca but was always up for a challenge and got the hang of it quickly. She also bet her grandson $50.00 that she would be texting within a month. Jewels took the bet and lost. Unbeknownst to Jewels, Beau was firing up her computer every night to hone her texting skills.

Jewels was drifting off to sleep, still smiling after reading Beau's text. He then remembered he had purchased a lotto ticket with the change from Beau's bingo winnings. He slowly pulled himself up from the sofa and started looking around for the ticket. He finally came across the ticket balled up inside his jacket pocket. He sat back on the couch and checked the lottery website for the winning numbers.

Jewels did not react immediately but suddenly jumped to his feet and began jumping from his sofa to the love seat, then back to the sofa. He uttered not a word, but silently screamed out loud. "Yesssss, yesssss, yesssss!!!!!!!" He screamed. This went on for about 15 minutes.

Jewels screamed, the silent scream of nightmares. It was just above a whisper, with an occasional squeal in between. It was late, so he didn't want to wake up the entire neighborhood. He also didn't want anyone to know he'd won, at least not yet. He debated whether he would call Beau to let her know. He figured it could wait until the morning. The last time he called Beau in the middle of the night, she didn't talk to him for a week. He promised to never do it again. This was important enough to wake her up, but he never knew with Beau. Finally, he collapsed on the couch in total exhaustion.

"I won! I won the freaking lottery!" he said out loud. "I won! I won 17 million dollars. I must be dreaming! Nope, I'm not dreaming, because the TV is on, and I'm watching it! I am not dreaming. This is real life and I'm not dreaming." Jewels paces the floor to ensure he is vertical, he is awake, and his mind is not playing tricks on him. This was a sensation that was so foreign to him that he wondered if he had lost his mind. He decides to say a prayer to center himself. "Father in heaven, please give me the strength to enjoy this moment without driving myself insane. You have given me this wonderful opportunity, but right now I'm on the verge of a nervous breakdown. If this moment is really real, please send me a sign. If you're too busy to send me a sign, I'll take your silence as my sign that this moment is real, okay? Okay God? Okay, good night. Oh, and thank you."

Jewels falls asleep with the lottery ticket tucked inside his Thom Browne loafers, folded neatly inside his Cervelt socks, with his laptop on top of his shoes, covered by his jacket, his belt, and a photo album. This would be the night that Jewels put the top lock on his door and places a chair behind the door. After placing his trusty hammer next to the couch where he decides to lay his head, Jewels fell asleep.

Reverend Charles and Family

Catherine, Chase, and Cerise Charles finally did it! They finally outdid themselves! After years and years of various punishments, privileges being taken away, banishment to their rooms, electronics bans, curfews, and various other low-level, teenage family crimes, the Charles girls had finally, collectively committed something so unbelievably scandalous that even their mother couldn't help them out of this one. They really blew it this time.

It began innocently enough. The Charles girls were very excited about Chase's 18th birthday. Catherine and Cerise would be turning 18 next year but were just as excited for Chase as they were about the prospect of turning 18 themselves. The twins and Chase were in the planning phase of Chase's birthday. It had to be phenomenal! It had to be colossal! They were determined that Chase's party would be talked about for years to come.

The Chase girls prepared the guest list, which included everyone they knew. There was a buzz in the air leading up to the big event. Everybody was in a festive mood leading up to Chase's big day—everybody, that is—except for the Good Reverend. Pastor Charles was not happy about it at all. He didn't mind that his daughter, Chase, was having a big party for her 18th birthday. He didn't mind that her younger sisters would expect the same treatment for their 18th birthdays next year. He didn't mind the toll it would take on him and his wife, nor did he mind the price tag for the party, which was nearing twenty-five thousand dollars. The Good Reverend didn't mind that he would have to keep a close watch to ensure the festivities did not involve alcoholic beverages. The idea that there would be many people in his home that he didn't particularly care for, didn't bother him one bit. The only thing that gave the Good Reverend cause for pause was his image, his character, and how this would all play out amongst the Board of Trustees and the Bishop.

The thought of an awkward exchange in front of these holy men made the Good Reverend shiver. His family was by no means perfect. His girls are good girls, but they live in an unpredictable world, full of would-be sinners. Pastor Charles did a daily run through in his mind of every possible snafu and how he would handle it. He even thought of cancelling the party altogether and taking his family on vacation instead.

After months of trying to change everyone's mind about the party, he finally gave in. The girls had to promise to be on their best behavior and control their friends. All of them. Of course, the Charles girls quickly promised to keep the party in check. They had also promised they wouldn't get tattoos. The three of them designed their own tattoos, featuring a bogus family crest, a bible, in case they were ever caught, a pair of Chanel sunglasses, the heart eyes emoji, and their initials emblazoned in the sparkling crest. All of this was done using fake IDs. They also promised their dad they would not get their ears pierced, so all three had belly rings. Never would they ever drive the family cars without permission. That's a discussion for another place and time.

While everyone was running around at the Charles home, decorating, and setting up tables, the Good Reverend spent most of his day praying for a tsunami to hit right before the party was to commence. He prayed for an ant invasion, a hot water heater malfunction, and a roof collapse. While he prayed and prayed for a miracle, the party was ON!

The DJ dropped by the house to set up his equipment and test out the system. Pastor Charles snarled at him as he walked by. The party planners arrived shortly afterwards and began stringing mirrored balls from one end of the house to the other. A balloon delivery truck pulled up, and soon there were hot pink and soft pink balloons everywhere.

When the dance floor arrived, Pastor Charles headed for the medicine cabinet. He emptied three headache tablets into his hand and gulped them down with water. By 6pm, the house looked like a nightclub. The only thing missing was the crowd.

Chase, Catherine, and Cerise were upstairs getting dressed. The three of them were giddy and ready to party. Catherine and Cerise busied themselves with Chase's hair. They talked and talked endlessly about the evening's affair.

Mrs. Charles walked from room to room, making small adjustments here and there. She couldn't be happier for Chase. Mrs. Charles was a very good mother to her girls. She took great pride in their school achievements, their wonderful spirits, but most of all, how very loving they were toward each other and everyone around them. She strives to make sure the girls experience as much normalcy in their lives as possible. The last thing she wants to do is suppress them with too much discipline. She often worried that the stigma of being "PKs" would place too much pressure on her girls.

The Charles girls are natural beauties, but their parents don't want their lives to be clouded by the "pretty principle." They want the world for their daughters, but they don't want the girls to rely on their looks to make it in life.

Mrs. Charles made her way back into the kitchen. She was so happy that they were able to hire the most sought-after caterer in the city. The food smelled heavenly, which was crucial when determining the success of a party. Chef Kayla and her staff had their game faces on. They had prepared all the girls' favorites. Soon the party guests would be chowing down on chicken and beef sliders, chicken fingers, and chicken wings with a side of ranch, blue cheese, and Sweet Baby Ray's BBQ sauce. There was an assortment of salads for Cerise, the vegetarian. The chef prepared a chef's salad, potato salad, broccoli salad, ambrosia salad, and a huge kale salad, Cerise's favorite. The fryers were full of fries and onion rings, and the back counter contained sweets and pastries of epic proportions. There were chocolate cupcakes, red velvet cupcakes, a three-tiered lemon cake, lemon cupcakes, brownies, lemon bars, chocolate chip cookies, New York Cheesecake, and a mound of pralines.

Mrs. Charles was really pleased with the chef and her staff. She exited the kitchen to check on her girls and to get dressed. The Charles girls were all done-hair and makeup-superb. Catherine and Cerise were putting the finishing touches on Chase. Cerise was so impressed with their work. "You look like a supermodel!" she squealed. The girls chatted and took endless selfies. Their laughter was so uplifting and inspiring that it gave the house an electric charge. Mrs. Charles walked in on the chatter. The twins stepped aside, revealing how very beautiful Chase looked. As Chase stood looking at her reflection in the mirror, she looked so very grown up. Her party dress was a pale pink velvet form-fitted beauty. It was enhanced with rhinestone jewels around the wide cuffs. Her rhinestone choker was perfectly matched to her earrings. Her sisters arranged Chase's hair in the perfect up do to showcase her outfit. Mrs. Charles embraced her girls with both excitement and pride. "Okay you two, now go and get dressed," she continued. Chase shooed them out of her room. Catherine and Cerise danced out of Chase's room, stopping only to demonstrate their best twerk moves for their mom. Mrs. Charles laughed hysterically as she bombarded her girls with throw pillows.

Chase stood staring at her reflection. She could hear the house filling up with her friends and family downstairs. She sat on her bed and began sending pics of herself and her sisters to their friends.

Catherine and Cerise began the daunting task of not overdoing it and outshining Chase on her big day. After all, the two of them together were way more stunning than most people could handle. At least that's what Cerise thought. The "daring duo" were certainly a force to be reckoned with.

Most people didn't know how to take the twins. The two of them purposefully set out to make everyone around them as uncomfortable as they could. They loved the idea that most people couldn't tell them apart and used every opportunity to keep others in the dark. Chase was the only person who knew one from the other. Since the twins are monozygotic, they share all of the same genes. The only difference in their appearance is their height. Catherine stands at 5'10 inches, and Cerise is half an inch taller. Other than that distinction, the twins are impossible to tell apart.

The Reverend and Mrs. Charles stopped trying to figure out which twin they were dealing with since the girls mastered the art of deception. The easiest way to figure out who they were dealing with was by their actions.

Chase had always been the big sister, so she knows her "lovelies" best. Chase nicknamed her siblings "Lovely" and "Lovely" when they were little girls. She thought they were the cutest things she had ever seen and always noted how very beautiful the twins are. Chase was so proud to be the big sister to the twins and was the first to protect them at all costs.

Catherine and Cerise agreed to dress down and not upstage Chase on her big day. Of course, this was a tall order, but they would figure something out. The twins loved dressing alike as it increased their intimidation factor. They delighted in making everyone around them wonder which twin they were talking to, and they almost always stomped the unsuspecting target. It was a dangerous game to play at times, but it never stopped them.

The twins once took a singular job at McDonald's just to see how long it would take the other employees to know the difference. This ruse lasted almost a full year. They made a lot of money, taking double shifts and even came close to becoming shift manager. When Pastor Charles caught wind of the mind games being played by the twins, he made them both resign. That little stint landed them "on restriction" for an entire month, and they had to take turns washing the family cars every weekend.

Today would be different for the twins. They wanted nothing more than to see their favorite sister win. Today would be Chase's Day, so the twins selected their basic black jumpsuits for the occasion and paired them with their favorite Jordans, bedazzled, of course. They settled on a subdued hairstyle as well. The twins wore their hair down with a simple part down the middle. It was hard to play down the twins' beauty. No matter how understated they dressed, they still outshone all others. The Charles girls radiated the kind of beauty that always turned heads. Big sister Chase led the charge with her subtle but flirty easiness. Fortunately for all three of them, they were smart enough to pretend they weren't aware of how pretty they were, as it kept them from getting a beat down by less attractive, more aggressive girls. It helped them make friends easily and gave them a sprinkling of humility. They knew this line of thinking was a total contradiction and lacked logic, but it worked for them.

The twins went downstairs without any fanfare, a first for them, and began mingling with the guests. They were always a big hit with just about everyone they met. "Of course, there were a few exceptions, but who cares about that?" Cerise would always say.

Catherine and Cerise greeted each guest as "their mama raised them right" and they circulated until everyone felt welcome in their home. The twins were mindful to ask the caterers and wait staff if they needed help with anything. They were raised to be respectful, helpful, and kind. The fact that they were also conniving and sneaky at times is another story.

Catherine's cell phone buzzes. It's Chase, and she's ready to make her grand entrance. Catherine grabs Cerise and they head over to the DJ. The twins take the microphones from the DJ then make the announcement in unison.

"And now, ladies and gentlemen, please turn your attention toward the staircase!" All the guests turn toward the stairs and wait for the next announcement. "Ladies and gentlemen, please welcome the greatest sister on earth, Chase Charles!!!" the twins proudly scream. Chase begins her descent down the stairs, all the while smiling and waving. Chase is a more refined version of her sisters, but she, too, has her moments.

Chase breezes through the crowd of her adoring fans and haters, leaning in for air kisses when appropriate. Many offer hugs and well wishes as she works the floor.

The party is well under way, and it's lively. It's the kind of party many will relive for years to come. The chef had to put out more food as the guests feasted on the delicious offerings. The food was so good that many of the guests booked the chef for their next event. The crowd mix was exciting as well. Chase and her sisters invited the "un-heard-of-crowd," "the in-crowd" and the unexpected guests that normally don't get invites. This vibe was good for the girls' PR as well as good chatter. Just like the Good Reverend suspected, a few knuckleheads were caught drinking, but the Good Reverend invited a few deacons to "handle" any riff raff before the bishop could catch wind of the situation.

The DJ let loose with a great mix of oldies for the old school, funk, pop and line dancing songs to get everyone involved. The twirling disco balls gave the house the feel of a nightclub. They danced, they ate, they partied, they took selfies and then they did it all over again. This party was a hit!

Toward the end of the event, Catherine, and Cerise whisper to Chase to meet them in their bedroom. Knowing how mischievous the twins could be, Catherine gave them both a stern look of retaliation if they tried anything. The twins promised they weren't up to anything, so Chase agreed to meet them after her last guests were gone.

When Chase entered their room, she gasped at the sight of their latest additions. The twins were super enlightened when it came to decorating. Their room was a mix of both their tastes.

Their ceiling was covered with pale purple night lights, galaxy lights, and shooting stars. This gave the room a dramatic, dark feel. There were oversized sofas that merged into twin elevated beds. There were electric swings hanging from the ceiling at opposite corners of the room. The swings were attached to the ceiling by purple ropes and embellished with lavender flowers.

Chase could just imagine the two of them swinging in sync. How they managed to get the Good Reverend to agree to this latest installation was beyond Chase's thoughts. But then, it was probably Mrs. Charles that they tricked into this move. Either way, it was "cool as hell," she thought. Chase plopped herself down among their million and one pastel pillows, waiting for the torture to be over. Cerise and Catherine could hardly contain themselves when they handed Chase a sealed envelope with her name on it. Chase thanked them and pretended to head for the door. "Noooo!!!" They both yelled. "You can't go! You must open it now while we watch you," Cerise laughs. "Okay, okay." Chase laughs as she opens the envelope to see that it is full of lottery tickets. "You guys!!!!! How did you get these?" Chase looks around to be sure no one is watching. She gets up and closes the bedroom door. "Are you guys crazy???" she asks. "Daddy will kill us if he catches us gambling." "That's why we're not going to tell him, now are we?" Catherine responds without missing a beat. Chase looks at them, still shocked that they got her one of the sneaky gifts she asked for, all the while wondering how they managed to pull it off since they were underage and not allowed to buy lottery tickets.

"Well, I have to admit, I am impressed that you guys got them, and I am going to have so much fun with the scratchers!" she says, holding the tickets close to her heart. "In case you hadn't noticed," Catherine says, admiring her fresh manicure. "We also snagged 10 Lotto lines for you."

Chase gasped for air, "no you didn't!!!"

"Yes, we did!" the twins reply in unison. "No, you didn't!!!" Chase replies.

"Yes, we did!!!" the twins repeat.

"How? How did you get these?" Chase asks. "We know people," Cerise slyly says.

Catherine pulls three coins from her pocket and all three girls' squeal in delight. This was their chance to play the scratchers game and try their luck at winning. "I've got a winner!" Catherine cheers! "Three whole dollars!" The girls applaud her big win. They continue scratching when Cerise decries, "Winner, winner, chicken dinner!"

"Well, I just won another $10.00," Chase announces. The girls are in scratcher's heaven while they shush each other in between scratching their cards.

"Y'all better hope we don't win anything big." Catherine warns. "Well, it's too late now," Cerise whispers.

"Stop playing Cerise," Chase says, with a playful pat on the arm.

Cerise does not respond but stares at the lottery ticket in her hand.

"Cerise, stop playing," Chase says, with an undertone of disbelief, but mostly hopeful that she's playing around. Cerise continues looking at the card and begins reading the directions on the back. "Stop playing, Cerise!" Chase says, almost crying.

"You know how Cerise plays, Chase." The look in Cerise's eyes should have been fair warning of things to come. "Come on keep scratching Catherine says and continues scratching her tickets."

"Hand to God?" Chase asks Cerise.

"Hand to God!" Cerise replies. "You just won eleven million dollars."

"I just won eleven million dollars?" Chase says, shaking her head, indicating she wanted no part of those winnings.

"Well they're your tickets, birthday girl, Cerise says, matching Catherine's tone," Cerise shoots back.

Chase snatched the ticket from Cerise's hand, then reads both sides of the card. The twins sit there motionless. After a few ticks, Chase looks at the twins, "Daddy is going to be so mad!" she says.

"He sure is," Cerise agrees.

"Well, what are you going to do?" Catherine asks.

"What do you mean, what am I going to do?" Chase asks with an edge now in her tone. "It's your ticket, birthday girl," Cerise says, matching Chase's tone.

"Oh, I see now," Chase says, shaking her head at the twins.

"So, the two of you want to abandon me and make me the fall guy," Chase continues. "Don't do the dance of the devil twins with me you little two headed monsters!"

"Well, it's your birthday and he likes you better than us, Chase," Cerise whines. "Besides that, you know how much Daddy hates gambling!"

"Yes, I do know! Don't you remember the sermon he preached about gambling just a few weeks ago? He'll kill us!"

"Oh yeah, I remember now," Cerise says. "I was falling asleep during that one, but I remember," she suddenly remembers. "Wasn't the Bishop there to hear him speak?"

"Man, oh man, oh man," Chase says with a huge head shake.

"I remember the bishop speaking with him after that sermon about the perils of gambling and how it destroys families," she continues.

"Ouuuu, Daddy's going to be SOOO mad," Cerise says in despair. "And he's going to be so disappointed, mad and disappointed" she finishes.

Cerise begins to cry at the thought of their dad being this upset with them. "Don't cry, Resie," Chase says, beginning to cry herself.

"Don't cry, Chase don't cry Resie," Catherine says, comforting her sisters as she begins to cry as well.

The girls are terrified of the wrath they will face once the Good Reverend hears the news.

Around 2AM, Chase awakens to find her and her lovelies spooning like they did as children. She was instantly transcended into their childhood. The three girls were inseparable and so happy to have each other. Chase felt so blessed to have her little sisters and always protected them. She decided a good night's sleep was in order. The news of a winning lottery ticket was a lot to take in after all the planning for the party and the party itself. Things would look better in the morning, she thought. She also thought she deserved a hunk of that chocolate cake that did not get touched during the party. Chase sneaks downstairs and slices a hefty piece of cake and pours herself a giant glass of milk to wash it all down. She sits in the middle of the bed along with her Lovelies and proceeds to eat every bite.

Shortly afterwards, Chase returns to her bedroom and tries to will herself to sleep. She figures a good night's sleep will help to sort out what needs to be done and things would be clearer in the morning. She also thinks about tearing the ticket into a million pieces. "How apropos" she laughs.

At one point, Chase finds herself, up and staring at the ticket with a pair of scissors. She is toying with the idea of destroying the ticket to avoid the wrath that would surely come down on them all. She quickly abandons that idea and heads to the bathroom to flush the ticket down the toilet. Just as she's about to enter the bathroom, determined to flush the winning ticket, a vehicle alarm sounds off which startles her so badly, the ticket flies out of her hand and slowly floats downstairs into the foyer. Chase races down the stairs, scoops up the ticket and high tails it back to her room. She jumps in bed, barely touching the floor and pulls the covers over her head.

Between the sugar rush of the huge slice of chocolate cake, the overall excitement of her over the top but fabulous party and her overzealous attempt to somehow undo what has been done with that damn lottery ticket, Chase falls asleep. Unfortunately, her sleep is filled with an ongoing recording of the Good Reverend droning on about personal catastrophe, moral and financial ruin and the father of all guilt trips—The Sermon on the Mount—"you cannot serve both God and money."

The sun awakens the twins with the brightest light beaming down on them. Under normal circumstances, the twins love and welcome the sun. Under present conditions, the twins want to crawl out of bed and crawl under it. They quietly crept over to Chase's room. To their surprise, Chase was already awake, showered and dressed. She decided not to wake her lovelies but let them sleep before they had to face the music.

The twins quickly shower and are dressed in a flash. Cerise had convinced Catherine that Chase was planning to rat them out. Catherine didn't believe Chase would do such a thing, but these were desperate times. Desperation causes people to behave outside of their character, so the twins had to prepare for anything.

The Charles girls met downstairs at the dining room table. Everyone is exhausted and hungry and begin scavenging the refrigerator for party leftovers. As the girls prepare their meals, the Good Reverend and Mrs. Charles make their way into the family dining room. Chase began laying out food for everyone to partake in and pours coffee for her parents. All this activity takes place in complete silence, which triggers the hairs on Mrs. Charles' neck. The girls were always animated, always talking, always texting, always complaining, and giggling about one thing or another, but this morning they were eerily quiet. The energy and spunk that spews over from this trio was replaced with magnified, deafening, uncomfortable quiet.

The Good Reverend is deep in thought as well, which is his usual M.O. in the morning. He always uses the mornings to pray, meditate, and get inspiration for his next sermon.

Mrs. Charles spoke about the decorum and grace of Chase's party. She commends her girls for how well their guests behaved and how wonderful the party was overall.

The Good Reverend's family felt a mini sermon coming, but surprisingly, he simply thanks his family for not embarrassing him and for keeping the party controlled. They all wait for the lesson, the connection, or the reflection. When the sermon didn't come, Chase stands up and suddenly blurts it all out. "Daddy we are so sorry to have to tell you something!" The Reverend and Mrs. Charles look like they are about to faint. Mrs. Charles holds her breath, waiting to hear what Chase had to say.

Catherine and Cerise lower their heads and hold on to each other.

"We, I mean I...I...I asked my Lovelies to buy me some, some, (now sobbing), lottery tickets for my birthday since I was turning 18, and since 18 is the legal age and all, and, and, (now shaking and crying uncontrollably) we didn't mean to, I mean I didn't mean to, to, to win, but I accidentally won Daddy, and, and, and I know gambling is a sin Daddy, but I just wanted to see, experience what my friends were talking about, and, and," Chase completely breaks down. With a little more composure, she continues, looking her dad square in the face. In a more controlled voice, Chase completes her confession. "Daddy, I'm so sorry to disappoint you and Mommy. I didn't mean to bring shame to the family, and I take full responsibility for this mess."

Cerise chimes in. "And I would like to commend Chase Charles for taking responsibility for this family crisis as she should because this was all her fault." Chase and Catherine, both give her the death stare for her backstabbing ways.

Mrs. Charles lets out a huge sigh of relief. "Thank God, I thought she was going to tell us she's pregnant!" The Reverend Charles does not speak but leaves the dining room and heads for the living room. No one follows him and no one speaks.

Mrs. Charles consoles her girls as she knows how horrible they must feel. Letting their dad down is the worst feeling ever. The sisters and their mom all embrace each other while they wait for their fate. Chase, now remembering the smart Alec remark from Cerise, pops her in the head for good measure. "What???" Cerise yelps after the pop. "No sense in all of us getting in trouble and getting thrown out of the house!" she continues.

"No one is getting thrown out of the house," Mrs. Charles utters. "Right Charles?" raising her voice and throwing it toward the living room, "I said no one is getting thrown out of the house, right Charles?" she continues.

The Charles household falls silent for quite some time. No one says a word for what seems like an eternity. The girls don't know what to make of their father's silence.

Is this really the end for the Charles family? The extended silence tears the girls to pieces. They had not cried like this in ages. Even their mother couldn't console them.

The Good Reverend finally appears in the doorway. He speaks very deliberately while addressing Chase—"I can appreciate your willingness to come forward and acknowledge your sinful act. I can also appreciate your taking full responsibility for willfully ignoring my teachings about the ills of gambling. What I do not appreciate is the collective defiance!"

"Oh, Lord, please help us!" Mrs. Charles wails. The pain in Mrs. Charles' voice startles the Good Reverend. He looks at his family with shame and with sympathy. With a deep sigh of disgust, he asks, "Where is the ticket?"

Chase steps forward and hands the ticket to her father. She keeps her head down, avoiding eye contact with him. Pastor Charles studies the ticket for a while, carefully reading both sides. He looks at his family, then speaks without changing his expression nor his tone.

"This ticket indicates the winning amount is eleven million dollars, is that correct?"

"Yes Daddy" the girls respond in unison.

"So, this is an eleven million dollar winning ticket?" he continues.

"Yes, daddy it's a winning ticket and I checked the internet site to be sure," Chase admits.

This news is a lot to take in, but the Good Reverend closes his eyes, and with outstretched hands, reaches for his family and yells out loud, "Thank you Father! Thank you!"

The Charles girls and Mrs. Charles run to the open arms of their father and husband. He plants a kiss on the forehead of each of the girls and gives Mrs. Charles one great, big hug and a kiss.

Chase asks, "Does this mean you're not mad at me, Daddy? And we still get to live here?" Cerise asks.

"Of course, you all still live here," Pastor Charles replies.

"But what about the bishop and the congregation?" Catherine dares ask. "What about them?" The Good Reverend replies.

"We can do a lot of good with this type of money. Everyone will look upon this blessing favorably. Blessings come disguised in different forms. A blessing is a blessing, and we can't always question why God chooses to disguise his blessings. In this case, he sent his blessing by way of 7-11. God bless the 7-11!"

Corporate America

Christmas time in corporate America meant fat bonuses for the executives. Fat bonuses for the executives meant the talk among the executive assistants, junior assistants, and administrative staff was about securing a great Christmas gift from their bosses. The best gift being cold, hard cash! The CEO and top executives are paid their regular salaries, receive stock options, and are additionally rewarded with short-term incentives or bonuses. This year's bonuses mean **everyone** will have a good holiday.

The company was doing exceptionally well as the revenue growth was at its peak. The purchase of a new corporate jet was a sure sign of a performance-based perk. This year's bonuses would be through the roof!

The assistants busied themselves with the distribution of the year-end reports, closing out payroll, paying past due invoices, and other mundane tasks that were keeping them from their last-minute Christmas shopping. Soon the office would be closed for a full week. The Chairman gave everyone the week off with pay! Instant messaging was raging! The assistants speculate on what they believe their individual bosses will give them this year. The executives never collude on what they will give their assistants so this, too, is another layer of excitement and anticipation.

Every year, beginning in December, the bonus bug is in the air. The energy level is continuously shifting throughout the company in anticipation of what could be. This will certainly be known as a banner year for the company and the topper is the company chairman is featured on the cover of the top four business journals in the country.

Instead of visions of sugar plums dancing in their heads, brochures of new cars, high-end fashion catalogs, and travel sites are being exchanged with the idea that these dreams will be realized within hours. The buzz permeates the air and continues until the checks are distributed and the offices are emptied out. This year would be no different, except for the additional bonus of a week's vacation.

It is a casual Friday and half of the executives had already started their vacations. Many had flown out of town to spend the holidays with their families. The remaining bosses and assistants would be treated to a wonderful lunch, compliments of the company.

The food is always catered by the restaurant, The Third Floor—a popular restaurant located on the third floor of the building. The Penthouse Suites is a loyal customer and fan of the restauranteurs and they prepare a feast for the company no matter what the occasion. The restaurant owners have a prepared cheat sheet in which the chefs have become fully familiar with. The meals include the individual needs of the executives and staff. Food allergies are taken into consideration and favorites are plentiful. This attention to detail is why the Third Floor is the company's favorite. The Penthouse Suites is known for its generous tips and the restaurateurs would always receive a generous tip, aside from the cost of the libations.

The staff expected generous portions and a great assortment of food, which they planned to share with their families. Everything the Penthouse Suites did was done to excess. An in-house holiday party for the staff was treated no differently than the offensively expensive, lavish parties the company hosted for their clients-tycoons, royals, and hoi polloi.

Like clockwork, the food arrived. The wait staff was ushered into the formal dining room which is usually reserved for top-level executives and their guests, but today was all about the Penthouse employees. The Chairman wanted the staff to enjoy themselves and opened the very private "Chairman's Armory" to all. The Chairman's Armory was so named by the famed former Chairman who was currently serving a well-deserved term at Allenwood. *Apparently, the former Chair would have plenty of time to figure out why he found it necessary to peel off an additional four million dollars for himself, purchase two condominiums-compliments of a hidden company fund and bankroll a very high-functioning gas station on top of his seven-figure salary. In addition to his salary, he received several bonuses, incentives, a company car, and access to the company limousine, to name a few perks. Why he felt the necessity to help himself to the corporate piggy bank was anyone's guess. At any rate, he would be spending his holidays playing team sports with his other tax-evading friends.*

The aroma of the various dishes permeated the office as the team completed the set up. The chafing dishes and white tablecloths gave the occasion the usual upscale flair-befitting a Penthouse Suites affair.

The staff slowly make their way into the lobby and the connecting wait area. The rooms are filled with expensive silver trays, stacked with a variety of Godiva chocolates; decadent, succulent brownies, an office favorite; spiral glasses filled with gourmet popcorn; meticulously formed mounds of cashews, pistachios, and macadamia nuts. There are silver ice buckets filled with "Bling" water. Hand-blown glass Christmas cottages are filled with glitterati candy and miniature chocolate candy bottles filled with assorted liqueurs. A temporary bar was set up, complete with professional bartenders and loaded up with top-shelf liquor.

The lobby is decorated by the professional holiday tree trimming service that placed five separate trees around the office suites. Each tree is decorated more beautifully than the next. The lobby tree at the entrance of the lobby is decorated honoring the Chairman. It is all done up in Swarovski crystals and gold twinkling stars. Its beauty is unmatched. Upon arrival, every visiting guest must have a jaw-dropping reaction to its presence.

The second tree is located near the reception desk and is just as elegant as the Chairman's tree. It stands eight feet tall and it, too, is decorated with Swarovski crystals but with silver mirror slivers. The dangling mirrors send quicksilver flashes of light all around. This tree's presence must mesmerize everyone with its stunning beauty. It is not only beautiful, but it is supposed to symbolize the brilliance of the minds that represent the company.

The third tree is a tribute to the company's well-known insignia. The Penthouse Suites logo is emblazoned throughout the tree and brilliantly displayed. The tree decorators hung a thousand bulbs on this one tree, making certain the company logo could be seen from every angle. The Penthouse Suites logo is not only stamped on every bulb, but each letter is carefully traced with tiny rhinestones for that extra "look at me!" The double-layered icicle lights put a finishing touch that is stunning.

The fourth tree is the company gifting tree. It is decorated with all the products from the company's boutique stores. The tree is decorated with miniature treasure trunks, and at the base of the tree there are wrapped miniature keepsakes as well as full-size holiday treasures from around the world. The gifting tree is always full of the most wonderful surprises. At least eight of the employees will be the lucky recipients to find the treasure trunks which contain crisp 100-dollar bills. The company spares no costs when preparing the gifting tree. It's The Penthouse Suite's way of giving back to those who help make the company so successful. The gifting tree grows more generous each year. The Penthouse Suites issues gift cards of various denominations to all staff members during holiday time. This year, every employee receives a five-hundred-dollar Visa gift card, a one-thousand-dollar American Express gift card, and a mixed assortment of coffee shop, candle shop, candy shop, cigar boutique, and department store gift cards to purchase gifts for their loved ones.

The fifth tree proudly stands at twenty feet and faces The Avenue outside. This tree is for the world to see. It is shamelessly displayed upon a pedestal, giving it an additional 5 feet as it soars to reach the lobby's 40-foot ceiling. This tree is the company's show pony, decorated to show the numerous Fortune 500 companies that line The Avenue that the Penthouse Suites is Top Dog! This tree is wired with high voltage lighting that can be seen for miles around. The tree screams, "Try and Take Your Eyes Off Me!!!" The bulbs are all made of platinum, and the tinsel is a mix of cubic zirconia and Majorca pearls. It's a very vulgar display of wealth, but "flaunting it" is part of the corporate games. The object of the game is to show all of Wall Street how your company kicked ass all year. Mel and her crew would begin their search for the rarest and most beautiful ornaments immediately after the holiday season. Every year is an opportunity for the staff to surpass all expectations from the prior year. Everyone in the office is counting on them to distinguish the Penthouse Suites from all others.

The assistants the Chief Operating Officers, Head Controllers, and all of the other "in charge types" are way more fascinating than the stuffy executives they work for. Mel is the ringleader of all the assistants. Her official title is Director of Office Affairs, but Melanie Steele is everything to everybody in the office. Mel is the head of personnel and, by far, one of the smartest women employed by Penthouse Suites. Mel is not considered an executive, though she occupies a single-panel small office that faces The Avenue.

Mel worked her way up the ranks through dedication and loyalty to the company. She is well respected for her work ethic and can-do attitude. All the assistants love and respect her as well.

Mel was upbeat on this day. She played an integral part in the preparations for the day's activities. She was carrying an envelope with the names of all the assistants written on it. The envelope contained $20.00 bills she collected from all the assistants and three members of the administration staff. The members of the administration staff fell under Mel's authority as well, so the two limousine drivers and the mailroom clerk are part of Mel's department. She collected their portion of the collective pot, as she did every week like clockwork. Mel purchased Mega Million lottery tickets for the administrative staff every week for the past two years. Executives were not allowed to participate in the lottery pool. After all, they were all millionaires already.

The object of the game is to *become* a millionaire.

The support staff plays the lottery faithfully. Every Friday afternoon, Mel passes out copies of the numbers to the assistants and administration staff after purchasing numerous tickets from their collective pot. She was certain to include every one of the support staff, even when they were on vacation. Mel would spot the vacationing co-workers, making sure everyone had a chance to win.

This was the staff's eleventh Christmas together. They are a very tight-knit group. They celebrated birthdays, anniversaries, weddings, baby showers, bar mitzvahs, bat mitzvahs, Taco Tuesdays, and Fireball Fridays together. They had poker nights, fight nights, pajama parties, charades, and various non-specific socials. They competed in corporate games, representing the Penthouse Suites in various sporting events.

This crew is as close as can be without being family. After Mel had collected from her crew, she headed over to the swanky smoke lounge in the basement of their building. The smoke lounge is a symbol of Corporate America's corruption in Mel's estimation. As she entered the "Smokey Room," as she called it, she could feel the eyes on her. Eyes, she felt, of salacious, corrupt men who had surpassed Father Time but considered themselves players. Mel felt nothing but contempt for them. She was deeply disturbed by their entitled ways. The fact that she wasn't allowed entry into the "Back Room" of the smoke lounge literally burned her up. She could make purchases from the smoke lounge but couldn't enter the "Back Room." What disturbed her more was the fact that the owner of the smoke room installed a lit catwalk from the entry door to the cashier. The rest of the room was dimly lit, giving off a club vibe. The catwalk allowed patrons behind the famed Amber Wall of the Smoke Room to ogle and stare at every woman that went down there to make a purchase. Mel's disdain for the patrons behind the Amber Wall was fueled by one thing, and one thing only-wealth. Mel is really disturbed by the uneven distribution of wealth in the world and in the US, but most of all-the men who work in the towers along The Avenue. Male domination and outrageous salaries, only awarded among the Ivy Leaguers' players, was more than she could bear. The smell of cigars, warmed brandy, and the smug laughter of suited men beyond the Amber Wall made the trip to the Smoke Room a chore, but it didn't deter her.

Being privy to salaries, incentives, bonuses, and all other extras was part of Mel's duties. While feasting on leftover filet mignon and unopened champagne, Mel rationalized her role as a means to an end. A big perk that came as part of her job is that Mel is welcomed at some of the finest places in town. Everyone knows Mel from the Penthouse Suites. Her position with the company has solidified some of the best contacts all around the world.

Her department was responsible for the payroll, purchasing company cars, travel plans, hotel stays, executive gifts, gifts for the wives of the executives, their children, and grandchildren.

Mel and a couple of assistants would spend days trolling through Neiman Marcus, Tiffany's, the Cartier Store, the Rolex Store, and many quaint specialty boutiques, all in the pursuit of the perfect gifts for the millionaire executives and their families. Shopping for millionaires gave Mel and her staff an appreciation for living well. Many trips to the out of the way, little known, rich people's haunts, proved to be a lesson in total indulgences. After all, doesn't everyone need a porcelain elephant with dark, emerald, green eyes? The eye sockets were filled with real emeralds. Mel and the assistants had become immune to the desires of the rich. They would faithfully begin their quest for whatever indulgences were on the lists. They, nor the sales associates blinked as they traipsed through the stores in search of mink lined socks whose fur could be removed during the summer months so the remote-controlled temperature cube inside the hidden pocket can be activated to cool off the feet.

The sales associates knew exactly where to find the one-of-a-kind remote controls that locked every door, turned on the house alarms and lights throughout the house, started the coffeemaker, opened the garage doors, turned on the TVs, and started the bathwater.

Mel and her staff became real pros at pretending to not be impressed. They would take turns handing over the company credit cards with the look of extreme boredom. Once they were in the back seat of the company limousine, they would crack each other up with the details of their latest adventure.

Mel and her staff also learned a very important fact about the rich. They learned the rich only spent time with people who could influence their wealth. Knowing that the executive would never befriend the lowly admin workers or any of the staff members that didn't have an office facing The Avenue. Oh no-no-no, hell no. Mel and the underlings forged deep meaningful relationships with one another. Mel and her staff a commonality to forge deep, meaningful friendships with each other.

Mel was also tasked with finding the best and most experienced decorators to procure the perfect furnishings for the lobby and all the executive suites. She hired a local artist to paint murals in the lobby, the Chairman's Armory, the executive lunchroom, the boardroom, and the legal library. The result was breathtaking. The walls were adorned with painted scenes straight out of a museum. Some walls were finished with silk wallpaper, while other areas received velvet treatments fit for a king. The Penthouse Suites became known for its own opulent suites. At least once a day, staff workers from other floors would take the elevator up to the suites to get a glimpse. The offices were featured in several magazines for being one of the most extravagant workplaces. Mel had to admit, she loved that distinction.

Being in this environment drove Mel. It forced her to be the best, to want the best. Her ambition would drive her to push her team as well. She wanted more for the assistants as well and convinced them all to participate in the lottery pools.

Mel's personal life was fueled by her ambitions as well. She was once engaged to a very successful man. She was very much in love with him and looked forward to the life they would eventually have together. Mel and her fiancé, John, had it all. Good looks, good jobs, and a great future together. Mel and John would soon find that their eternal happiness would not come to fruition. Mel was completely blindsided by an executive from the West Coast. Mel fell head over heels for the guy. It was an uncanny attraction that came out of the blue. Mel was supposed to help the transplanted executive find an apartment, rent a car, and basically help him set up his new life.

As with everything she does in life, Mel gave this task her unyielding attention to ensure this man would be happy with his transition.

Maxwell Minor was hired for his vast knowledge of the industry, his undeniable, highly sought-after list of contacts, and his overall achievements for many Fortune 500 companies.

Recruiters from other firms had been wooing Maxwell to get him to join their companies as well, but he entered into an agreement with the Penthouse Suites. He always wanted to live on the West Coast, and the Penthouse Suites provided him with the perfect opportunity.

Maxwell was thrilled to work for the Penthouse Suites, and it certainly didn't hurt that Mel was probably one of the most attractive women he had ever met. Her warm smile and devotion to the company were also very refreshing. Maxwell Minor had heard about Mel's upcoming nuptials, so he was very careful to respect her and not overstep his boundaries.

The two became fast friends as they tooled around the city, going from one apartment listing to another. Since the company was paying for Maxwell's lodgings for the next two years, Mel wanted to be sure he was comfortable. She only took him to the finest locations. Success came quickly for the duo in their search for the perfect location. Mel insisted that his new address would automatically ring of class and sophistication. Two Fallon Drive would become Maxwell's new abode. The unit is located on the 39th floor of one of the swankiest high-rises in the Marina. The views were simply breathtaking. The apartment overlooks the city from his living room, and his bedroom view showcased the beautiful waves of the ocean.

Maxwell's furniture was delivered one week to the day after his move. Mel was busy with the movers and the placement of Maxwell's furniture while he took calls from 3 different cell phones. Mel was quite impressed with Maxwell's business acumen and his ability to navigate effortlessly on a worldwide scale. She watched in awe as he conducted a series of phone calls while navigating deals in English, French, and Portuguese. She was beginning to understand why he was so sought after. Maxwell from her perspective, was a business genius, a statesman, and dreamy as hell.

In the meantime, Mel was bogged down in wedding plans that couldn't seem to come together. She cancelled one appointment after another, trying desperately to finish getting Maxwell set up. She was being pulled in so many directions that she would sometimes forget to eat.

One evening, she dropped by to deliver some of Maxwell's belongings that were inadvertently delivered to the office. Maxwell answered the door while taking calls, of course. Mel was so used to Maxwell being on the phone that she went about her work and did what Mel does. She began unpacking the boxes as she pulled them in on her trusted dolly. Mel was no stranger to Maxwell's apartment, so she went about the task of finding a place for his belongings. In the midst of fussing over the details of Maxwell's new place, Mel came across a picture of a very pretty woman, encased in a crystal frame, Mel was transfixed on it. She continues unpacking Maxwell's boxes until they are empty. Maxwell continued his conversation as he paced the floor of his apartment. He motioned for Mel to have a seat and poured her a glass of wine.

Maxwell finally ended the phone call and immediately apologized, "Mel, I am so sorry to keep you waiting so long. I hope you're hungry because I ordered food from Ronnie's." Mel was surprised when Maxwell realized how much she liked the food from Ronnie's and took the time to order it for them. She was still consumed with the vision of the woman in the frame in her mind. "Who is she?" Mel thought. "Why do I care who she is?" she continued.

When they finished their meal, Mel helped clear away the containers and glasses. "I can't thank you enough for all your help, Mel. I never could have done all of what you've done here to help me. You made this transition so easy, and I can't thank you enough."

Mel smiles, then reluctantly gathers her things to leave. She so wants to inquire about the woman in the picture, but quickly remembers it is none of her business and it would be presumptuous for her to ask. Maxwell walked Mel to the door, then remembered he had something for her.

"Oh, just a minute, Mel," he says as he heads to his bedroom and quickly returns to the living room to hand Mel a small bag. Mel took the bag from Maxwell and quickly thanked him as she headed out.

The idea that she wouldn't have a reason to continue popping up at Maxwell's apartment made her a little sad. The token of his appreciation inside the bag was a further indication that the attraction Mel felt for Maxwell is not reciprocated. Somewhere along the line, Mel seemed to forget she was engaged to be married and she shouldn't be pining over this guy anyway. Mel admitted to herself she was smitten with this man, but obviously he felt differently. Obviously, he was in love with the woman in the frame.

As she made it to the elevator in Maxwell's building, Mel figured she'd suffered some temporary insanity. Why on earth was she so infatuated with someone that was off limits, out of her league and involved with another woman? What was even more insane was that she knew she was engaged and planning her wedding, but she was willing to risk everything in her life with John to pursue this uncontrollable attraction she had to Maxwell.

As Mel reaches her car, she realizes she's crying. She wipes the tears from her eyes and begins assessing what's happening. She feels both hurt and confused. Mel knows she really loves John and wants to marry him. She also knows she has feelings for Maxwell but was just shut down. She had a feeling Maxwell might be attracted to her as well but was holding back because of her engagement. She couldn't reconcile her emotions and spent a fretful night trying to get to sleep.

The next morning, Mel called and checked in with John, making an excuse to cancel their plans for lunch. John was used to Mel's sometimes hectic schedule and happily agreed to meet with her later. Mel wanted more time to figure things out. She was always in control of her life and didn't like the head space she was in.

Saturdays were usually reserved for breakfast with John and lunch with her girls. On this Saturday, Mel detoured and headed to Burke Williams. There she would find the peace and tranquility she desperately needed. Without hesitation or looking through the service menu, Mel orders the Hunter's Retreat. The best thing about this treatment is its ability to relax the body into complete surrender. When they were done with you, you truly had nothing left.

Mel could only describe the Hunter's Retreat as a symphony of warm water drizzling all over your body, followed by a mix of warm body scrubs. The initial drops of water and warm body scrubs dripping down from the pristine silver pipes were the most wonderful feeling you could ask for. The silver pipes would spray warm misting water into the air which Mel describes as liquid sun. The entire room would fill with the fog that would transform the room into a warm sauna. As the fog slowly cleared, the silver pipes would then release a series of aromatic hot oils from head to toe. This was followed by another deluge of steamy warm water that continued until all of the oil and scrub were removed. The last step was a stream of warm water that was so incredibly soothing, it was hard not to ask for a second session. The machine then doused the entire body with another dose of a fragrant oil. The aesthetician quietly slips into the room and calmly explains how she will rub the oil all over your body. The beautifully fragrant oil covers the entire body, then she wraps you in a warm towel. Mel was then led to the quiet room where she would sit and sip ice cold lemon water. Her eyes were covered with a soothing mask.

Mel fell asleep in the quiet room, not knowing or caring that the morning had slipped away. She woke up two hours later feeling more clear-headed and refreshed.

On her drive home, Mel stopped at her favorite yogurt shop to treat herself to a large yogurt with all the trimmings. No sooner than she sat outside to relax and enjoy her yogurt, who does she see pulling into the parking lot but Maxwell Minor himself. There he was, looking all fine and handsome and fine. He didn't see Mel, or maybe he didn't recognize her since she was dressed down in sweats and tennis shoes. This look was a far cry from how she dresses for work. Mel adjusted her sunglasses and watched while Maxwell ordered yogurt and waited for him to exit. She debated whether she would invite him over to join her or ignore him and pretend she never saw him. She sat and debated the two choices, repeatedly, "speak or ignore—speak or ignore— speak or ignore—speak or ignore," she battled. While she was busy fighting with herself, Maxwell arrived at her table and was standing over her. A very embarrassed Mel asked Maxwell to join her. From there, it was on!

Mel and Maxwell began an affair of epic proportions. Hiding the affair was another story.

After the initial tryst that began at the yogurt shop, Mel and Maxwell began to see each other every chance they got.

Maxwell pursued Mel with everything he had. His pursuits left Mel tingling at the very thought of him. Her feelings for John had not changed and she had every intention of going through with the wedding. John was her best friend and the love of her life, and he would be the man she walked down the aisle with.

Maxwell, on the other hand, represented the intangible dream lover that women fantasize about. Mel knew in her heart that the two of them could never really be. She decided she would ride the train until it derailed or until she came to her senses, whichever came first. Though their connection was undeniable, Mel kept her wits about her and enjoyed the ride.

After months of justifying the physical connection to Maxwell and lying to John and everyone else that almost caught them, Mel realized she wasn't emotionally available to either man in her life. Mel ended the affair with Maxwell and called off the wedding. John tried to forgive Mel for her indiscretions, but the deception was too great.

Chilled champagne in a salted ice bucket, sleep, therapy, yoga, Hunter's Retreat sessions, yogurt, girlfriend circles, cooking, and more therapy, helped Mel realize she was infatuated with the idea of Maxwell, and he took full advantage of her as he sensed she was suffering from exhaustion. Maxwell represented the man she could never have. Men like Maxwell were very aware of the power they held over women, so of course he seized the moment to take full advantage of her. Well, that's the conclusion Mel and her cohorts came to. He probably slipped her a mickey, they thought. Her friends were sympathetic and supportive. Some scolded her, feeling she knew better, while the more progressive ones felt she deserved one last fling before her nuptials.

Whatever drove her decision, Mel willingly allowed herself to be drawn into this world she was obsessed with. Here was this man who was extremely handsome, very smart and a business maverick. What choice did she have?

Mel paid the ultimate price for her decision. That decision caused her to lose her fiancé, the man of her dreams, and it almost cost her job. When the Chairman learned of the illicit affair, he came down hard on Mel for her poor choices. The very thought of the person whose job it was to uphold the company's Code of ethics was guilty of the highest form of inappropriate behavior. The person entrusted with upholding the organizations' standards by preventing any potential conflicts of interest was embroiled in the middle of this potential legal compliance scandal. Mel was expected to be let go ...

Mel was grateful to retain her position with the company, but she later learned that Maxwell didn't receive as much as a reprimand. Mel imagined she was the topic of discussion when "the boys club" had their little secret meetings. What was even more disturbing was Maxwell's admission that his wife, hence the woman in the crystal frame, was an international spokesmodel whose parent company was in Dubai. She spent half the year in Dubai and would join Maxwell in the U.S. at the end of the year.

Mel was mortified to learn she had been played. It didn't matter that she was a player as well, but the thought of this credent playing her was too much for her ego. When the job reinstated her after a brief suspension without pay,

Mel resumed her position and her tribe of assistants fell in behind her. They were a very loyal group, and they needed Mel's leadership.

Mel returned to the office with a treasure trove of lottery tickets. She went directly to the copy center to make copies for the assistants. Once this task was completed, she distributed copies of the tickets and wished them all good luck. The mega lottery had rolled over several times and the jackpot was up to three-hundred-eighty-million dollars.

The office was set to close right after the luncheon, but Mel had to ensure all the office lights were turned off, the coffee machines were turned off and cleaned, the hallway doors were closed, and the alarms were set. Her final task was to program the Christmas tree lights to turn off at 5 AM every morning. The trees would be illuminated throughout the holiday season. The Chairman wanted everyone on Corporate Row to know the Penthouse Suites are Number One Twenty-Four Seven. Mel turned off the lights and exited the Penthouse Suites to enjoy the holidays.

Bossed Up

The Friday drawing of the lottery caused quite a stir. The proprietor of the "Smokey Room" stood tall in front of his store as the local news reporter announced that the winning lottery ticket had been purchased at his establishment.

Meanwhile, a group of twenty-six ladies, two limousine drivers, and an office clerk were piling into their chartered minibuses. As they entered the buses, they immediately noticed the space was full of balloons, shaped like dollar signs. Each bus had a full bar, and everyone wasted no time turning up.

Mel organized what she claimed would be her final act for Penthouse Suites employees.

She pulled out all the stops. The party buses were two-tiered, Mercedes luxury wagons. The stripper poles were illuminated, and the sound system was awesome.

Mel led the toast, "Nothing but the best for the best," she said with raised glass. "Here! Here!" the party crew agreed and completed the toast. Mel could finally relax in her comfortable leather seat, and she did. Mel's hunch that they would all share in the lottery winnings one day had proven correct. Mel and her tribe of assistants were the lucky and only recipients of the 380-million-dollar lottery ticket. The group abruptly quit their jobs and set out to do "whatever the hell they please!!!!"

As the lottery winning ex-assistants left The Penthouse Suites for the last time, the executives could do nothing but applaud. Some of them were annoyed that their assistants all left so abruptly, but it didn't matter. Mel's last official duty for the company was supplying them with a new Mel, Melinda Stevens. She would oversee recruiting and hiring new staff.

Mel and the ex-assistants formed a conga line into the waiting party buses and that was the last the company executives heard from any of them. It was a beautiful moment.

Tailor Song

It was prom season and Tailor Song was booked, captivated, and knee deep in his work. "Tailor is busier than a one-legged man in an ass kicking contest!" This is the phrase Tailor used to convince anyone listening how very full his schedule was. Someone once used this phrase on Tailor, and he thought it was the most truthful yet hilarious way to describe his very abundant life.

Tailor Song was a gifted tailor whose workmanship brought in clients from miles around.

Businessmen brought their expensive suits to Tailor to achieve the perfect fit. He would cut a pair of slacks to precision. The tailoring on his jackets was spot on. Presently, the dry cleaners where Tailor worked was overrun with prom dresses-needing Tailor's finishing touch.

Tailor was the head seamstress/tailor at Goodson's Dry Cleaners. He was the only seamstress/tailor at Goodson's, but he wanted to give the impression of a seamstress/tailoring empire. He believed the competition should always feel threatened by his excellence. Tailor should be looked upon as the one "bringing flawlessness and exquisiteness to the game." This was another favorite phrase Tailor loved to espouse.

Tailor is exactly how he presents himself, which, to most, is a bit much. His friends view him as the "last word," and Tailor places a period at the end of that sentence. To know him is to party with him. Life is one endless party for Tailor, AKA "Tay Tay." He would only allow a select group of friends to call him by his childhood name. That distinction came after proving themselves worthy of his trust and their honor.

What probably sets Tailor apart from most seamstresses/tailors is his uncanny ability to try on, mark, and fit everything he touches. Tailor had to "feel" what the client wanted. "You can't send a garment out into the universe without experiencing the life it will have. These clothes must make a way for themselves once they hit life's runways."

Tailor is by no means ordinary. For one thing, he believes he lives his life in halves.

Though he is only 25 years old, he believes he has already lived half a life that needed adjusting. After 25 years of living a dull existence that brought nothing but fear and unhappiness to him, he emerged and was reborn into this perfect mix of man-woman-child-adult that could live a life without boundaries. His reward for living the first 25 years in a full depressive state was this newfound spotlight of a life that he earned. The fact that he is still chronologically 25 has no bearing on Tailor's logic, as he believes his new life was gifted to him to live as he pleases.

His belief that he is half man, and half woman is the complexity he lives. Even though he only possesses male genitalia, he knows he has the heart of a woman. He often mentions that his hair is both curly and straight, which, in his mind, is another indication of "halves life." He believes he was given a crown of controlled beauty, which would be the envy of every woman and every man who would want to touch it. The fact that Tailor was half Asian and half American further added to the notion that his "halves life" theory was his destiny. The topper to Tailor's theory of living life in halves is his idea that he is always both joyful and melancholy.

Tailor realized early in life that it would be in his best interest to be interesting. Since there was no counter to being interesting, he thought just being interesting would have to do. His gift of seamstress/tailoring came quite by accident. Tailor was once a young theatrical actor. He was in line to become the youngest stage actor to play the lead role in Westside Story. When he was awarded the part, he played the role to perfection. The theater extended the performance for an additional three months. Soon, Tailor was a working stage actor in high demand. He landed several roles and almost always the lead role. Although Tailor loved the attention and accolades of the theater, the money was not that great. One day, while practicing backstage, the London Fog coat, which was essential to his character, was ripped from one end to the other. Tailor was not about to go on stage with a ripped jacket, so he immediately grabbed the coat and headed to the wardrobe department. Once there, he began the meticulous task of restoring the coat to an acceptable place. When Tailor finished sewing it up, the coat looked better than it did before.

Everyone was amazed by Tailor's skills. It was so good, the theater director offered Tailor a handsome sum to become the theater costume curator.

Tailor leaped at the opportunity to become a young theater curator. From his perspective, the position paid way more money than he was making as a stage actor, and he could use the theater wardrobe to supplement his own. The theater company had some of the most sought-after pieces Tailor had ever seen. Several pieces were donated by larger theater houses at the end of the season. More importantly,

Tailor loved the idea of the coveted title, "Theater Curator." Tailor was already thinking of ways to always remind anyone listening that he was a theater curator. It had such a nice ring to it.

Tailor worked the Curator gig for the next three years. By the end of the third year, he was over it. Tailor was ready to move on. Someone mentioned the gig at Goodson's to Tailor, and he snatched up the "Help Wanted" sign in the window as he entered. Tailor made decisions quickly and without looking back.

His friends were very surprised by his abrupt exit from the "dream job that he absolutely loved with all his heart and soul." What his friends didn't know is that Tailor had not lost his love of the theater. Tailor had lost a part of himself in the theater. For someone who was living his life in halves, he certainly couldn't imagine living half a life. It wasn't the same thing. "No siree, no never, not me!" Tailor pledged. After several tawdry affairs, Tailor exited the theater-stage left.

Looking back, Tailor's first suitor sat front row center at each showing of "Death of a Salesman." Tailor was transfixed on this lone, lovely stranger who he believed was perfectly suited for him. Tailor believed the stranger was 30 something, impeccably groomed, super handsome, and apparently available. Tailor studied the young man night after night during the show, then stalked him a little afterwards. Not wanting to appear desperate or too forward or pushy, Tailor did what Tailor does. He found the young man during intermission, then set his plan in motion. Knowing the stranger was an avid fan of the theater, Tailor offered to take the stranger on a backstage tour. Of course, the young man jumped at this opportunity, and so did Tailor.

Months into their love affair, Tailor had grown weary of Sean's infatuation with theater life. At first, Tailor thought it was so cute, but the cuteness had worn off, and Tailor was ready for the next contestant. He began seeking out his next victim, um, lover.

"This time," Tailor thought. "I'll be more selective."

Tailor began to self-analyze and concluded that he could be a little superficial at times. He also addressed the issues that some close friends brought to his attention. He didn't realize that his over-the-top personality and insistence that his guy had to be "at least as handsome as he, if not more" was asking for too much. All this thinking gave Tailor a headache, and "headaches were not good for beautiful people. They made them wrinkle their foreheads. Besides all that, his kind of beauty should not be lost on ordinary-looking people," he concluded. It was Tailor's sincere belief that extraordinary-looking people, like himself, were placed on the earth to give beauty to an otherwise plain-looking, strange-looking society.

Imagine that.

Tailor was quick to find Sean's replacement, and he came in the form of a member of the ballet. The ballet featured a principal dancer cast as Puck in George Balanchine's, A Midsummer Night's Dream. Tailor was so excited about the "new boy" in the black tights, he could hardly contain himself. Since Tailor was the costume curator, he was introduced to every member of the ballet company upon their arrival. While the theater manager showed the group around the theater, Tailor grabbed the arm of "the new boy" and gave him a private showing.

At first the new boy was taken aback at Tailor's forwardness, but he slowly settled into a puddle of putty, just like Tailor imagined he would. Tailor certainly had a way with people. He was extremely handsome, and that handsomeness had a persuasive power instilled in it. That deadly combination worked every time. At least it did for Tailor. Most people assumed Tailor was very smart, as he transmitted an heir of scholarly knowledge. His fondness for Jeopardy and a good memory were the source of his knowledge. People often thought him to also be trustworthy, kind, and seductively mysterious. Having these virtues projected on him only "bratted" Tailor out more so. He knew he possessed an overwhelming charm to lure in his victims, um lovers. He had great success finding the perfect man, but he was continuously in search of a better one.

Tailor and his beautiful "Ballerina Boy" were quite the pair. They were both so uniquely handsome, it was difficult to decide which one to stare at. "Ballerina Boy" was blonde with piercing blue eyes, while Tailor's mane was jet black with a slight curl to it. Tailor has a very chiseled jawline and smooth, creamy skin. He also possesses the longest natural eyelashes any woman would die for.

The two of them turned heads everywhere they went. Tailor enjoyed every second of every moment they shared in the spotlight. For Tailor, the extra attention only validated what he already knew, "physical attractiveness is better."

When the ballet company's time was up at the theater, Tailor had a decision to make. It wasn't much of a decision for Tailor, as he had already prepared his farewell speech for his beloved Ballerina Boy. The two of them embraced and "Ballerina Boy" was gone. Tailor would always hold a special place in his heart for his "Ballerina Boy" that is, until the next pretty face arrives.

Tailor's next victim, um, suitor, was the perfect match for Tailor. Edward was his name and he approached Tailor first. Well, he didn't approach Tailor, rather he pursued him.

One day, Tailor unexpectedly received four dozen yellow roses backstage. A card was included but not signed.

A few weeks later, Tailor found himself signing for a stainless-steel wine cooling refrigerator. Tailor was both fascinated and infatuated with the idea of this unknown stranger. At the end of the week, the champagne arrived with two beautiful flutes. The message in the champagne glass read:

"The mood has been set for a lovely evening of wine and song. You have the wine and I have the song. Please say yes!"

Tailor smiled and felt a sudden self-consciousness that was difficult to overcome. The adrenaline release had him breathing breathlessly, and his heart was fluttering. This was a new feeling for Tailor. He waited for the next clue to arrive from his secret admirer. Each day, he grew more and more restless.

At the end of another day of flawless curating, Tailor was confronted by an imposing figure. Tailor turned around, and there he was. Not very tall, not very dark, and not very handsome at all. Tailor was neither amused nor impressed. He stared at the odd stranger, arms folded and ready to unload. The odd-looking figure cut Tailor off before he could speak and asked him to accompany him to the waiting black sedan at the back of the parking lot.

"Well now, that's more like it!" Tailor exclaimed as he sauntered toward the sedan. Tailor enters the moody Town Car and sits like a young schoolboy across from his newest suitor. He doesn't speak but slowly drinks in his soon-to-be, new love.

Edward would be all Tailor imagined—tall, sophisticated, smug, stuck up, serious, smelling good, sassy, syrupy sweet, and a whole lot of other good words that start with "s."

Since the letter "s" was his favorite, Tailor would often use words to describe his sweet things that began with "s." He knew this was a weird quirk, but who cares.

The one thing Tailor was never inclined to do was to get involved with a married man. To take on a man with a wife was nothing he had ever encountered. He knew he was more beautiful than most women, but how would he compete against a natural woman? For the first time in his life, Tailor felt he was not up to the task.

Tailor gave Edward his word that he would never utter a word about their affair to anyone. Little by little, Tailor fell under Edward's spell. Tailor wasn't used to taking the less dominant role in a relationship. Edward was a natural leader, so Tailor just followed Edward's lead. Edward was very systematic in all that he did. He had to be to pull off the duplicitous lifestyle he was leading. Edward had to pretend and blatantly lie. It takes a grand level of scheming and deceit to pull off that kind of double dealing.

Besides "Driver," Tailor learned that Edward's mother knew all of his secrets and kept them close to her heart. She noticed early on that there was something different about Edward. Early interactions with Edward indicated a softness that grew as time went on. His mother often blamed herself for Edward's way, but over time she embraced his calm and gentleness. She realized Edward wasn't gay because of their closeness. They were close, and he just happened to be gay. They often laughed about it and settled into a friendship grounded in love and respect. Through the years, Edward and his mother spent time sewing, shopping, creating new hair styles for each other, gossiping, and sharing other interests as well.

Edward played his dual role well, but Tailor wanted more. "Maybe he didn't want more, maybe he wanted to be TheOnly," Tailor thought. Being number two and playing second fiddle is a foreign concept to him. He had these long awkward conversations with himself. "Do I want more for myself, or do I just think I want more for myself because someone else has him too?" There were no real answers to these questions, only more questions.

Tailor had a moment of clarity when Edward's wife called one day. She insisted Edward needed to come home immediately. Tailor could hardly breathe. He helped Edward dress, making certain there was no trace of Tailor on his person. In that moment, Tailor felt a chill so strong that he knew, in that moment, it was over. He stopped taking Edward's calls and refused all gifts thereafter. That chapter of his life was a closed one.

Goodson Cleaners provides Tailor with just the right amount of drama, comedy, and kickass wardrobe a girl could ever dream of. Goodson's caters to the upper echelon with expensive taste and some of the best pieces Tailor ever laid eyes on. Tailor is in his element when an exquisite piece is sent over for alteration. He would sometimes spend hours in the mirror admiring himself in the expensive sweaters, jackets, and coats. Every now and then, he would solicit the help of his co-workers to put on his own fashion show. He even managed to get the angry steamers to provide him with the "smoke machine effect" as he dances, gyrates, and pirouettes around the store. The crew got quite a kick out of watching Tailor do his thing.

One Tuesday morning. Tailor was alone in the store. He had just completed a full rendition of Diana Ross's, "I'm Coming Out!", all the while twirling and gyrating in a customer's beautiful, beaded gown. Mr. Johnson enters the store, laughing hysterically. "Excuse me, Mr. Johnson," Tailor curtly states. "I know you're not laughing at me!"

"Don't get yourself all twisted, Tailor. I'm not laughing at you," Mr. Johnson continues. "I'm laughing joyously! I just won the lottery!" he finishes.

"Oh, my goodness!!!! Oh, my goodness!" Tailor says, clutching his pearls. "Wow, you must be on a cloud!" Tailor shrieks.

"I'm just so happy, Tailor, I'm so happy," Mr. Johnson says, now gasping for air.

"Well, don't get yourself too worked up, Mr. Johnson," as he escorts the man to a chair. "Can I get you some water or something?" Tailor asks.

"Thank you, son, thank you," Mr. Johnson responds, breathless. Mr. Johnson wipes his forehead, which is beaded with sweat.

Tailor returns to Mr. Johnson with a cup of water and a towel to wipe away the sweat. "Thank you so much, Tailor," he says. "Now that I've calmed down a bit, let me show you my winning ticket."

Mr. Johnson pulls out the winning ticket and proudly shows it off to Tailor.

"You must be so happy Mr. Johnson. I'm so happy for you and your family," Tailor says.

"I am so very happy, Tailor, but there is no family. It's just me. My wife passed away many years ago, and I could never replace her. I don't have any children and no other living relatives."

"Well, I've never been this close to anyone that ever won the lottery, Mr. Johnson. Let me rub your head for good luck!" Tailor and Mr. Johnson laugh together as he stands up to leave.

"Wait, Mr. Johnson, don't forget your clothes," Tailor slides across the counter to pull Mr. Johnson's dry cleaning. As Tailor prepares to hand Mr. Johnson his clothes, he notices Mr. Johnson is slowly falling toward the floor. Tailor races over and catches him before he hits the floor. Tailor is pinned to the floor under the weight of Mr. Johnson's ample body. Tailor screams for help, but no one is around to come to their aid. Tailor manages to struggle to get his cell phone out and dials 911. He tries desperately to revive Mr. Johnson but notices that Mr. Johnson's eyes are fading. Tailor begins to cry as he feels Mr. Johnson leaving the world. Moments later, Mr. Johnson would become the first person to ever expire at Goodson's Dry Cleaners. At that same moment, Tailor Song became an instant millionaire. Tailor remained on the floor, clutching Mr. Johnson's left hand with his right hand, and clutching the twenty-three-million-dollar winning lottery ticket with the left one.

The Millionaire Express Casino and Resort

The marketing department worked tirelessly to bring the best shows, the best casino stores and boutiques, and the best restaurants to draw the highest of high rollers. This year would be no different. The Millionaire Express Casino and Resort would be the first to host an event of this sort.

The Millionaire Express Casino and Resort will host lottery winners from all over the country.

So far, the resort received RSVPs from everyone they invited. Sparing no expense, the casino offered the millionaires' top accommodations, which included the best suites, 24-hour room service, on-call valet service, and their own private chefs in the famed Glasshouse Restaurant that only seated twenty guests. The Glasshouse is known for its huge floor-to-ceiling windows, magnificent marble floors, glamorous cocktail bar, and thousand-count votive candles.

The invitees had to only show and share the amazing tales of their lives since winning the lottery. If they happened to do some gambling while there-well, that was another story. The casino is always open to anyone who wants to play.

Enter The Charles Family

The Charles family were the first guests to arrive. Their limousine, compliments of the casino, pulled into the circular and the paparazzi clamored to get pictures of this unprecedented spectacle. The Charles girls embarked upon the casino first, looking like three breathtaking movie stars. It had only been a few years since their big win, and the ladies looked better than ever. The Charles girls, now young women, were all decked out in ivory beige athleisure wear, furry beige jackets, and beige hiking boots. They wore dazzling sunglasses and flashed big, sparkling smiles. Their hair was styled similarly, which made it difficult to determine the twins from their big sister, Chase.

Mr. and Mrs. Charles were fashionably dressed as well, but not as flashy as their girls. The Good Reverend did not want to appear ostentatious as the Bible and his modest upbringing taught him all about humility. Anything showy was not his way. God had given the Good Reverend's family an opportunity of a lifetime. The time would not be spent buying overpriced, splashy, designer labels when understated, expensive, less obviously expensive clothes would do.

The Charles family made their way through the small crowd that had gathered. Someone said the hotel hired paid actors to stand around and go crazy when the lottery families pull up. Even if it were true, and it was, heads would roll if the casino marketing staff found out who let the cat out of the bag.

The Charles family was whisked away by security. The Good Reverend was anxious to write down his thoughts for his next sermon. Pastor Charles wanted to talk about the spoils of wealth. Since becoming a millionaire, the Good Reverend was eager to get out his new message of building wealth without being showy. The Good Reverend wants to shine a light on what being wealthy looks like from God's perspective. He explained to his flock that the wing expansion at the Charles family home gave the Good Reverend more room to expand his thoughts and allow for deeper thinking. His vision of generational wealth and retirement was his new mission statement. His shiny Rolex was a gift from his daughters, so that didn't count. He wanted to prove to others that the investment in his daughters' education would pay off one hundred times over. Enrolling them in elite universities would give them the best education and introduce them to very well-connected families. This would in turn produce some of the finest minds, and those great minds would be surrounded by great opportunities.

Enter Jewels and Beau

Next to arrive were Jewels Wright and his loving grandmother, Beau. Jewels and Beau arrived in a Hummer Limo Truck, fully loaded, just like Jewels ordered. The casino allowed the special guests to order their own ride to the resort, so Jewels hunted down a limousine specialty dealer. The rest is Hummer history.

Jewels jumped out of the Hummer, dressed for the fashion gods. He wore a black leather shirt, black wool slacks, and a pair of Louboutin Black Melon Spikes Chelsea Boots.

Jewels ran around the truck to take the hand of his beloved, Beau. Beau donned a smart navy blazer, navy turtleneck and navy wool slacks. Her shoes were crocodile leather, also in navy blue. Beau's monochromatic ensemble screamed elegance, and she knew it.

Jewels escorted Beau into the casino as though she were royalty. In his mind, she is.

Enter Tailor Song

Tailor Song and Company rolled up in a red Ferrari La Ferrari with a price tag of 1.4 million dollars. Tailor chose to provide his own ride to the casino so he could come and go as he pleases. After all, the financial freedom his winnings gave Tailor proved to be the fantasy life people only dream of. Tailor understood his fortune was also the tragic result of Mr. Johnson's untimely demise. As a true measure of his good character, Tailor hosted the fanciest and most ostentatious funeral he and Mr. Johnson's money could buy. With those odds, Tailor left nothing to chance. The world really is his "effen oyster!" he frequently says. His financial windfall will be fully enjoyed, and nothing is impossible. "And besides," Tailor reminds himself, "work is a four-letter word."

Tailor was not alone and never lonely. Along the way, Tailor met and fell in love with many. If he could only control the desire to find love, he would not get swept away so easily. He would then turn around and sabotage the relationship for fear that the right person might come along,

The Ferrari glistened in the daylight, but there was no movement from the driver or the passenger inside. Suddenly, the upward-swinging butterfly doors opened in synchronized slow motion. Tailor had the doors adjusted so he could make a splashy entrance for dramatic effect. Like two ninja warriors, Tailor and his passenger sprang from the vehicle, performing a perfect gymnastics style landing. They both then laughed hysterically at the looks on the valets' faces. This move never failed to crack Tailor up.

One thing Tailor always did was to reward those who served the public. After working many years in the shadow of others, Tailor would learn to change people's perception of him. He still wanted to have fun, and of course he did, but he also wanted to bring joy to others.

After completely startling the valets with his antics, Tailor gifted each valet with a crisp $100-dollar bill. The valets were a bit confused as there was no luggage to pull from the beautiful car. Tailor and his companion skipped their way inside the casino. After checking in, the two of them pulled into the men's store inside the casino, where they purchased matching outfits for the weekend.

Enter StCyR Peters

StCyR Peters landed at the Casino Heliport accompanied by his father, stepmother and his brother and sister. StCyR's interests included aeronautics, so this was his opportunity to venture into that world.

Shortly after winning the lottery, StCyR decided to take a chance at finding his father. His mother, Random, told StCyR about his father when he was 13 years old. Random wanted StCyR to know he had a father in the city, but she decided he was not for her. StCyR never questioned his mother about his father again. StCyR's wild imagination would often drift into a reverie of a dad so impactful, it would be days before he realized he dreamed it all up.

Random had given StCyR the Cartier watch and money clip Milan left in the apartment they once shared. These two items meant everything to StCyR. Growing up, he would often gaze at his heirlooms and wonder about his father.

StCyR used a portion of his winnings to narrow his search for his father. A single posting of the watch and clip on the right sites eventually led the father and son to an in-person meeting. StCyR bore no grudges against Milan; he just wanted to see who helped him carve out his DNA. He was anxious to see if he looked like his father, if they possessed similar personality traits, were they the same height, but most of all, StCyR wanted to be in the company of someone that knew his mother. He wanted to hear his father's side of why Milan left his mother. He was hopeful Milan would be open about his mother's plight as a young 16-year-old girl being pregnant and ending up alone. StCyR needed to know why Milan left them. He didn't care if they developed a friendship because of their meeting; he simply wanted answers.

The visual StCyR carried in his mind did not meet reality. When he rang the doorbell of Milan's home, he was suddenly overcome with emotion. He thought it might be better to turn and leave but argued against it. He made the effort to pursue this, so he choked back his fears and tears and just stood there, frozen.

When Milan opened the door and looked directly into StCyR's eyes, he began to sob. It was quite a sight. Two big men crying like babies standing in the doorway, staring at each other for what seemed like an eternity. Milan was overcome with emotion as the images of Random ran through his mind. There standing before him was the son born during a time of turmoil in his marriage to Babel. The resemblance to his mother was both undeniable and haunting to Milan. StCyR, on the other hand, wept the tears of the 14-year-old boy, suddenly left alone in the world as his mother left without him.

Babel felt the tears sliding down her face but abruptly joined the two of them, taking StCyR by the hand. She welcomed him into their home while Milan calmed himself and settled down. Babel's gentleness and soft smile were a welcome relief for everyone.

After finally gathering himself, Milan approached StCyR and Babel, who were seated on the couch and continued staring at him. Finally, Milan spoke, "I'm so sorry, StCyR. It's just that you look so much like your mother," he continued. Babel excused herself to allow the two of them to talk privately. There was an awkward silence that befell the room as the two men looked at each other.

StCyR noticed subtle gestures Milan made that mirrored his own. He also noticed that he and Milan had the same hands, the same dark eyebrows, and a small mole on the left cheek. Milan spoke first, "I'm not going to sugarcoat what happened with your mom and me. Babel and I hit a very rough patch in our marriage, and we were growing apart. I ran into Random one day and felt I needed her in my life. I take full responsibility for what happened between us," he concludes. "I want you to know that I genuinely cared for your mother; it's just that I was selfish and feeling alone, and she was there. I never meant to hurt her." he continued, "I desperately tried to find her, but she vanished, and I never heard from her again."

StCyR sat quietly for a moment without reaction. He could see the pain in Milan's face and could tell from his furrowed brow that Milan had a million thoughts running through his head. The silence between them was overpowering. Neither of them knew the words to exchange to ease the moment. StCyR silently wondered, "Where were you when I needed you?"

StCyR's thoughts were suddenly pulled in the direction of a young man entering the house. The young man was a little older than StCyR, but not by much. A young woman pushed her way inside from behind. The young man and woman turned out to be Milan's son and daughter, StCyR's siblings.

The young woman brushed past her brother and introduced herself, "Hi, I'm Greer, and you must be StCyR," she says, smiling and giving StCyR the once over. StCyR stood and extended his hand when Greer gently tapped his hand away and gave him a big hug, "What are you too good to hug your sister?" she laughs.

"Milan Jr," the young man says. "Don't worry, I won't hug you and make this all awkward like some people," Milan Jr. snickers. Young Milan stands staring at StCyR, noticing the uncanny resemblance between himself and his father. Other than StCyR's complexion, hair, and sunburst eye color, StCyR, Milan, and Milan Jr. all looked very much alike. They were all identical in height and body structure.

Greer, on the other hand, was the spitting image of her mother. Greer was the breath of fresh air the room needed. She took StCyR and Milan Jr. and hurled them into the bathroom. "Now go wash your stinky hands so we can eat," she tells StCyR and Milan. Looking startled, StCyR hunches and heads into the bathroom to wash his stinky hands. Milan Jr. watched Greer in all her brazenness, and immediately heads to the bathroom to wash his stinky hands as well. "Well, at least I'll get a reprieve from her for a while. Looks like she has someone else to boss around besides me," he continues. Everyone laughs at this exchange.

Babel had prepared a feast, just in case, so the family sat together to eat. Babel was more than prepared for StCyR's arrival. She was ready to provide StCyR with whatever was needed.

She knew she could never take the place of StCyR's mom, nor would she try. Babel knew whatever relationship was forged between Milan and StCyR, she would stand by them and act as a bridge for her family. Babel felt a kinship with StCyr. She knew she loved him the moment she met him. The love affair between Random and Milan is what brought Babel and Milan closer than ever.

StCyR and his family stepped off the helicopter and dashed inside the casino. Their arrival was met with little fanfare, but StCyR fulfilled a wish to see the city from an aerial perspective. The casino invitation did not limit their travel to the resort to ground travel, so he used this opportunity to fly.

Enter the Corporate Crowd

Mel knew better than to trust Post with the accommodations at the casino resort, but Post was adamant that someone besides Mel should take the helm and handle the details of this trip. Mel knew all of the former executive assistants and assistants were more than capable of arranging transportation from the airport, but what she didn't know is that Post had just returned from Carnivale in Rio de Janeiro. Post was so impressed with her visit to Rio that she arranged a parade float to pick them up from the airport. So much for spending their money wisely.

Not wanting to spoil the mood of the revelers, Mel takes a seat at the back of the float.

Even though the sun had set hours before, Mel sat perched with her Chanel shades firmly planted on her face. She watches with amusement as the ex-assistants dance to the piped in music from the float's sound system.

The float itself is a 30-foot monstrosity that resembles an old-fashioned circus big top.

There are tons of flashing, colorful lights illuminating the float and a collection of beads and trinkets dangling from the perches. Mel thought the circus tent was quite fitting for their arrival. The life-size carousel in the middle of the float held some of Mel's former coworkers. Others swung freely from the mini trapeze catch bars while the rest of the crew sat on assorted carousel horses, going around in circles as they all swayed and sang silly songs all the way to the casino.

The krewe was met by the casino staff who spent an inordinate amount of time unloading the mountain of Hermes Bags, Louis Vuitton Travel Sportage bags, Fendi, Coach, and Crocodile Duffel bags, stuffed with designer sweats, sneakers, scarves, hair extensions, assorted jewelry, snacks, lucky condoms, boxes of cigarettes, expensive chocolates, crossword puzzle books, and all of the things in life, none of them needed.

The boozy guests piled off the float and danced themselves into the casino and straight into the restaurant bar. Mel pulled up the rest, helping her fellow millionaires pick up their cups and tequila bottles along the way. Mel gave the valets a wicked smile as she slipped inside.

The Casino Lure

The next morning, all the millionaires were scheduled to participate in an all-exclusive breakfast where they would meet the casino's high rollers. This event was dubbed "Platinum Touch." This event would highlight the lifestyles of those who took a chance in life. By exploiting, er, illuminating the lives of everyday people who took a chance and won, the lottery industry would see a spike in lottery sales all over the country. The Millionaire Express Casino and Resort thought it would capitalize on the good fortune of ordinary people. The hook would be the lure of sudden wealth to the hopeful and curious. Videos and stills would be taken featuring the lives of the attendees before they took a chance and afterwards. This was touted among casino insiders as a great marketing strategy to bring in the common money.

By all standards, the breakfast was a huge success. The wait staff floated through the banquet room in their dress uniforms. The tables were covered with black and white tablecloths, and at the center of each table were crystal dollar signs. Each place setting was a glass square with the names of each guest engraved on the front of the square. There was silver, platinum and gold rock crystals carefully placed all around which gave the tables the appearance of a sparkling stars.

Every place setting held an open black velvet box with a gold satin lining. Inside the boxes were one-of-a-kind gold watches containing diamond hour markers, and each watch had the guests' names engraved on the back. The card read, "Compliments of the Millionaire Express Casino."

The guests were thrilled with the red-carpet treatment. They posed for the photographers, there to capture the opulence and fantasy of the event. The guests mingled and congratulated each other on their individual successes as the wait staff began to bring out the meal.

The food was prepared by some of the finest chefs around and nothing was lost in the presentation. The wait staff busied themselves with endless trips to the tables, piling on fresh salmon, salmon croquettes, giant shrimp on skewers, lady fingers, Bluefin tuna and caviar. The next course featured lamb medallions, chicken medallions, beef skewers, Otoro sushi, and Kobe Wagyu.

The meal would not be complete without a flurry of fresh vegetables. The wait staff placed delicate bowls of asparagus spears with garlic butter, mixed greens with pink lettuce, Yamashita spinach, wasabi root and La Bonnotte Potatoes all around the table.

Dessert was the guests' choice. They could choose from an array of ice cream flavors, Golden Phoenix Cupcakes, gourmet jellybeans, and LaMadeline au Truffles flown in from Connecticut. The wine list was endless, featuring the best champagnes in the world.

At the end of breakfast, the guests were more than satisfied. Some said they were dizzy from all the rich food.

At 2 o'clock in the afternoon, the guests were tapped to meet at the hotel ice bar. The photographers enjoyed snapping pics of the guests at the Ice Bar because the Ice Bar was so magical. Everyone that entered was awestruck at every turn. The Ice Bar did not disappoint. Upon entering, each guest is fitted with either mink, sable, fox, or ermine. There were fur replicas for those who preferred faux furs as well. Everyone was also given disposable hand warmers and insulated gloves.

The first stop at the Ice Bar was the "shots station." Even the glasses were made from ice. Fortunately, the shots hit the right spot and instantly warmed the guests, so they could continue the tour. The Good Reverend and his daughters did not partake but happily shared their hooch with the others.

Next stop was the Ice Lounge, specializing in warm drinks that warm the soul, or "liquid fire," as some called it. The drinks at this location were served hot and guaranteed to warm you from the inside out. The Good Reverend and Mrs. Charles ordered the hot chocolate for themselves and their daughters. When their parents' backs were turned, each girl received a nice shot of rum in their hot chocolates from the bartender. Those girls are such charmers.

The other guests filled up on chocolate drinks full of Baileys, hot peppermint tea full of vodka, full cups of Hennessy with hot coffee, and double espresso shots with liqueur.

The tour continued with the guests entering ice igloos illuminated with crystal chandeliers. The very spectacle of these igloos is beyond-beyond. The chandeliers inside dripped with beautiful multi-colored crystals. The Igloos are such a fun idea. The guests are treated to party drinks that are a swirl of bright colors, neon lighted ice cubes; and a large block of fiery sorbet is plopped atop each glass. A running board of flashing lights runs along on the floor of the igloo, and brightly colored, day-glow candy stir sticks add a whimsical touch to the set.

The Igloo drinks are delicious. Some were sweet, while others contained a mixture of sweet and salted rings around the rim. Some drinks had multi color lemon/lime rings floating at the bottom of the glasses.

There was another drink with gum drops swirling above the slushy liquid, and there were vodka-soaked sour belts lining the inside of the colossal glasses. The stir sticks were lollipops with Scotch centers. The stir sticks were used for all the brown liquor drinks, which were poured warm from a fancy kettle. The Charles girls assured their father they were only eating the "candy stir sticks." They also convinced him that the center of candy sticks was a chewy caramel. The group left the Ice Bar totally exhausted. They were a very happy group after the tour, but they were totally spent from the experience.

Millionaire Expose

There was one final event on the group's itinerary. Even though everyone was sleepy and hungover, the unfortunate assigned concierge promised this last event would allow them to relax. The happy millionaires were ushered into the casino theater where the next phase of their experience would happen.

The concierge gave each of the millionaires an assignment. The assignment was to go onstage and introduce themselves. They were to make a statement about how they would use their fortunes and how their windfalls impacted their lives. They all were to make a statement about how their fortunes have changed them and what they have done to help others. This information would certainly make for excellent footage to share with the next aspiring millionaires.

Beau and Jewels were the first to approach the podium. Beau was tired after the visit to the Ice Bar and was ready to hit the casino. She figured the casino noise would wake her up. Jewels pretended not to know that Beau just wanted to gamble. Beau pretended to care what Jewels was thinking.

Beau made it very clear that she would donate any money left from her fortune to the city schools once she departed earth. Beau was very big on education, and she had already arranged to have the school systems receive whatever was left of her winnings—as a token of her love for higher education. Jewels promptly collects Beau as she leaves the stage. Jewels had quite the buzz going from his visit to the Ice Bar and opted out of speaking about his philanthropic matters. He would later send a written statement indicating the donation of a community garden. Realizing the importance of fresh fruit and vegetables in the diet, Jewels donated a portion of his winnings to an inner-city garden. The garden would be tended by the residents of the community, and the fruit and vegetables would be distributed to the members of the community at no charge.

Beau and Jewels were met by a well-dressed agent of the casino and escorted out through the backdoor.

Next up was StCyR Peters. StCyR is a patron of the arts and announced he would be donating a total of one million dollars in total to the preservation and renovation of the museums of the City of New Orleans. StCyR loves his city and all that it has to offer. It gives him great pleasure to give back to "The City that Care Forgot." StCyR remembered reading that slogan and vowed to care enough to never forget the love New Orleans gave to him. StCyR's announcement was met with whoops and cheers. The loudest cheers came from the former assistants, who were quite blitzed from their time inside the Ice Bar. Many of them had also developed a big crush on StCyR.

StCyR was then escorted to the same exit as Beau and Jewels.

The remaining millionaires all recorded their pieces for the docuseries before being led through the exit. The next and last stop for the day was a rest area where they could all relax and receive their dinner information.

A Twist of Fate

Once all the guests reach the relaxation and reflection room, the room suddenly goes dark. Someone screams but is quickly muffled.

Simeon, the unfortunate assigned concierge for the day and the personal valet for the guests, cautions the guest to sit still and not to panic. Apparently, there was a blown fuse, and it would be corrected momentarily. The room remains pitch black, and all the guests are without their cell phones, as they were instructed to leave their phones and tablets in their rooms so they would not be distracted.

"Attention all guests, attention all guests, the problem has been identified and the lights will be restored momentarily," a calm voice announced. After a few moments and a little bit of movement, the lights come on to the relief of the guests.

The relief was short-lived. To the Millionaires' horror, when the lights were restored, they are shocked to see that all the casino staff are tied up and gagged and shuffled off into one corner.

The guests are confused by what they see. Was this some sort of joke? Was it part of the casino's itinerary—to scare its guests?

There were two men at the exit of the relaxation room and four others who quickly began to quietly circulate the room. All the men are dark figures with face coverings, gloves, and dark clothing. They're wearing what appears to be the dark colored casino jackets, but upon closer look, the jackets are not casino issue but a similar looking knockoffs.

Finally, a lone figure appears on stage and makes the following announcement:

"Ladies and gentlemen, may I have your attention, please. I'm going to make this simple request of each of you, and then you can continue with your journey. There are thirty of you in this room. Each of you will be transferring one million dollars to an offshore account by way of this very convenient kiosk terminal. For your added convenience, we have saved you all the trouble of accessing your money market savings, and investment account information. You need only to transfer the funds to the account number provided. Once we receive notification that the transactions have all cleared, you'll be free to go."

The guests show a mixture of emotions but sit in silence. The puzzled looks on their faces indicate they are still not certain if this is a joke. The man on stage continues, "This room is equipped with noise reduction wall tiles and the camera feeds have been temporarily re-routed. No one knows you're here. We'd like to do this quickly, so please step up to the kiosk and enter your information." The voice behind the mask is slow and steadied. The tone of the voice is menacing and serious.

"How do we know you'll release us unharmed?" Beau questions.

"If everyone does what they're told, you'll all be out of here. There's no reason for us to harm any of you. None of you have seen our faces, so there's no story to tell, no heroes. We're not taking your complete fortunes, only a tiny bit. We're not here for a slaughter, neither financial nor otherwise. We are only here to take what's necessary from those who are more fortunate than most." Then, with a very authoritative voice, he continues, "Now move!"

The millionaires are given their preassigned cards as they step up to the kiosk. Some of the guests are incensed, while others are disgusted and outraged. The very idea that their personal account information has been accessed by these unknown thugs is very disappointing.

As the millionaires step up to the kiosk, they reluctantly follow their captors' instructions. They really have no other choice but to cooperate. The thugs are armed, and the guests weren't. Total no brainer.

Mel is the last guest in line. As she steps up to the kiosk, she asks, "So what if I don't do it?"

The masked guy next to the kiosk pulls out his 9 mm and presses it against Mel's cheek. Through clenched teeth, he says, "Try me!"

Mel glares at the thug and refuses to step up to the kiosk. The room is rife with tension. Some of Mel's colleagues plead with her to just do what they say. Mel reluctantly gives in and performs the transaction. You could hear a collective sigh of relief throughout the room. Mel returns to her seat but spits on the floor at the feet of their captors before sitting down.

The kiosk booth is quickly rolled out of the room. Then, like clockwork, the men leave the relaxation room, one by one. The room is suddenly completely dark again, and no one moves.

Finally, Tailor speaks up, "Mr. Robber, are you still there?" After a few moments, the millionaires begin to slowly crack up over Tailor's question. Tailor slowly makes his way toward the light switch and flicks it on.

The guests all look around, relieved to be alive, and they check on each other and provide comfort to those they were emotionally disturbed by what had just happened. Mel cautions everyone to remain calm and to stay where they are. She checks on everyone in the room before going out to find security. After about 20 minutes had passed, Mel returns with security and the local police. Each guest is questioned by detectives and hotel personnel. The room was then meticulously checked for any identifying information to help with the investigation.

The Long Ride Home

The next morning, StCyR Peters, Jewels Wright, and Beau and Tailor Song sat quietly in the lobby of the Millionaire Express Casino and Resort.

Beau sits motionless while she waits for their ride to the airport. Jewels tries to get her to loosen up and count her blessings, but Beau wasn't having it. Jewels reminds her that the casino has insurance, and they would all be reimbursed once the investigation was completed. It wasn't the money for Beau, it was the principle. Beau is a woman of a certain age, and principles rule in that world. This incident shook her foundation.

Usually, Jewels could get Beau to laugh, but this was different. Beau's ego was hurt. No one had gotten the upper hand on her since her late husband, Earl Jewels Wright.

Earl's death left Beau consumed with grief. Beau was so distraught and lonely that Jewels' mother made the decision to have Jewels move in with Beau as a distraction and for company. Once Beau finally recovered from her loss, she vowed never to allow herself to let another man have that sort of power over her life, never again.

This experience angered Beau more than anything else. She couldn't wait to get home, where she could pray in the comfort of her home. She had so much to tell Earl that night.

The long white limousine pulls into the circular and Jewels escorts Beau inside. Beau takes Jewels' hand as always, and she proudly enters her chariot. Jewels stood looking tall and handsome with that big wide grin. He has so much love and admiration for his grandmother. He knows how she feels and would do all that he could to pull her out of the funk.

Beau sat in that limousine with her face perched, all set to pout the entire way home. She glances over at a grinning Jewels and can't help but smile as she adjusts herself inside the car. Jewels sits across from his grandmother and pulls out an assortment of cordials from his pockets. "Drinks, anyone?" he asks. Beau laughs hysterically as the limo pulls away.

Tailor Song, on the other hand, decides to throw a full on, total tantrum-styled, adult meltdown. He paces the casino lobby floor with lethal accuracy. Tailor was overwhelmed by the way they were robbed. Pacing allows Tailor to rage loudly, and the clack, clack, clack of his Louboutin's against the super shiny, marble floors could be heard from quite a distance.

This experience hit Tailor differently than the others. Tailor is reminded of the pain he felt as the school bus sped away each day. He is reminded of how small and helpless he felt at the hands of the young boys at school who tortured him daily. The boys at school learned of Tailor's diary he kept buried inside his backpack. Tailor's diary would tell the secrets no one was supposed to know. Once his secrets were exposed, his life became a living hell. It was bad enough he faced the cold, harsh stares of his peers and the constant taunting of the bullies, but even worse, he couldn't tell his parents any of it. Tailor's father would never understand his plight, nor would he ever defend his son. His mother was too whipped to go against her husband. She stayed in her place and pretended not to know. Even after Tailor confided in her, she kept pretending not to understand.

Stomping around the hotel lobby would help him push through and forget those days.

Tailor stomps and stomps until he realizes he is in step with the music playing in the nearby lounge. Once the rhythm of the music pierced his soul, he begins to sway, a little at first. As the music begins to draw him in, Tailor found his center and did what Tailor does. He begins gyrating and "working it out." Tailor's moment of pity and reflection of what was, was already done. He grabs his companion's hand, and the two of them boogie down to the lobby bar. After a few ticks on the clock, the pair emerge from the lobby bar with two big old fruity drinks, complete with umbrellas, colorful swirly stick candies inside the glasses, and a miniature bottle of rum turned upside down, affixed to the side of the glasses. Life just got good again for Tailor Song.

The valet had the butterfly doors of Tailor's Ferrari open and waiting. Tailor and his companion jump inside and ride off into the sunset. A few minutes later, Tailor and his companion pull back into the circular with Prince's "Kiss" blaring on the radio. Tailor lets his window down and hands the valet a couple of hundred dollar bills, lets his window up, then screeches off to his next adventure.

StCyR, his father, Milan, his stepmother, Babel, StCyR's brother, Milan Jr., and sister, Greer, met for breakfast at the casino cafe before their departure. Milan and Babel were philosophical about the cyber robbery and offer StCyR some advice. They had a suspicion this was an inside job based on the accuracy of the crime itself. Milan questioned the validity of the investigation, suggesting an FBI investigation. Milan figures the casino does not want that type of negative publicity. A crime of this caliber would garner too much negative publicity, so the casino quickly engages the local police department to wrap things up. The local law enforcement did not hesitate to clear the area and keep it all moving.

The casino staff was quick to wrap up the weekend for the millionaires. Things were set in motion to get the distinguished guests away from the scene of the crime and squash the memory of the event. It's pretty obvious the

Millionaire Express Casino and Resort owners are much concerned about the rest of the hotel guests finding out about the crime. The casino knew this type of targeted crime could potentially empty out hotel if the guests knew their personal information could possibly be compromised.

From Babel's perspective, the robbery appears to be a possible crime of opportunity. Someone on the inside had to be involved. To pull off a cyber-robbery inside the casino with a handy dandy money machine in tow, reeks of an inside job. The fact that this was all done without so much as a trace of evidence, no video footage, no witnesses to interrogate—is just too convenient. Greer and Milan Jr. sit and listen intently. They were in their rooms when the crime went down, so the story of the robbery was most intriguing to them. With Greer studying law and Milan Jr. studying psychology, both are very mindful of the events leading up to, as well as the events that occurred during the cyber robbery. Their field of study has them laser focused on the details as they listen intently to draw their conclusions based on the facts. They would also draw from Babel's experience as a marriage and family therapist. Somehow, her conclusions were often spot on. In the end, the entire family is convinced it's an inside job.

Milan is relieved that no one was hurt during the ordeal. He offers to contact the District Attorney's office once they were home, but the locals graciously declined. Again, the casino industry was not big on having a bunch of law enforcement hanging around. Many of their top tier guests did not want that type of exposure.

StCyR and his family walk arm in arm toward the Mercedes Benz Sprinter van that has arrived to take them to the airport.

The family shows much more appreciation for each other after this experience. They embrace each other as if they were all headed in different directions. StCyR particularly has nothing but praise for his family. During a time of crisis, his family is there for him, and that feeling is what he had craved ever since he lost Random. As the van pulls away, StCyR smiles the smile of a newborn baby. The knowledge of knowing how much this family loves him gives him the loving feeling he once knew with his mother. After all, he didn't choose this family; they chose to take him in and love him.

The former corporate office assistants came down the escalator, carrying on and reconstructing the moments of the robbery. They are a noisy bunch-rowdy, tremendously fabulous and exciting. They were all leading effervescent lives after working tirelessly to promote the lives of the spoiled Ivy League executives they worked for. Their new lives were so very entertaining as they quickly assumed the position of making the most of life. None of them were ever impoverished, but working with millionaires for all those years gave them a taste of the good life. It wasn't hard for any of them to assume a grandiose, larger-than-life existence.

These are mostly college-educated individuals that came from middle-income families. They feel a certain pride in helping to fashion the outcome of a publicly traded company. The former assistants played a significant part in the rise of the corporate giant during their tenure with the company. Their efforts did not go unnoticed, but the chairman and executives received the accolades as well as the big bucks for the success of the company.

Because they were stopped at the velvet rope of the corporate ladder of success, the former assistants were excelling at *"living' la vida loca!"*

Because they were unable to cross the lines of the velvet rope of the corporate ladder of success, they had a different relationship with money. They were very adept at investing in the right stocks, annuities, real estate, and bitcoin stock. They learned from the sharks how best to keep the money rolling in while they slept. They all took a vow to never work again. With Mel guiding them through the maze of investments, this group would live the life they only dreamed of.

Mel was like a life guru for the group. She is also their counselor, shoulder to cry on, babysitter, sister, mom, party planner, chauffeur, nurse, chef, etc. Mel always seems to have the right answers and was always ready to rescue.

It was no surprise that Mel lagged behind the crew, cleaning up the suites to ensure they would not be barred from future hotel stays. She stays behind to clear out the numerous empty bottles of champagne and to toss their receipts bearing coveted credit card information. Mel was careful to shred the receipts found in the suites, unplug, and retrieve cell phones and tablet chargers left behind, collect single shoes left beneath the beds, and scoop up sunglasses, reading glasses and handwritten notes, long forgotten. Mel is a "cleaner" by instinct.

To be sure they didn't head to the airport in a tractor or some other contraption that one of her eggheads thought would be "fun," Mel ordered the ride for their return trip to the airport.

Luckily, Mel caught wind of Bandeaux's brilliant idea to have a team of horses and stagecoaches pick them up. That little stunt only cost them twelve-hundred dollars to cancel.

A two-tiered motor coach picks them up to haul them off to the airport. As the bus pulls away, the Charles family steps into the lobby. The Charles family was lucky enough to catch a bird's eye view of two of the nuts on board the former corporate staff, mooning them.

Catherine, Cerise, Chase, and the valets laugh hysterically at the sight. Pastor and Mrs. Charles stood, opened-mouthed, in complete astonishment. The Charles girls could not contain themselves. The circus bus slowly pulled out of the hotel circular.

Catherine and Cerise stood side by side, as they often do, when Catherine suddenly and discreetly began nudging Cerise. Cerise knew something out of the ordinary was on the horizon, but this was better than anything she expected.

In a beeline heading in the direction of the twins were a set of male twins that fell right out of a model search. Catherine and Cerise are no strangers to men falling over themselves to chat them up, so they posted up and put on their best "not interested" faces.

The young men had an uncanny resemblance to each other as they arrived directly in front of the Chase girls. The one on the left spoke first, "We are sorry to interrupt but my brother and I just had to come over and introduce ourselves. By your obvious identical traits, it appears you are monozygotic twins, as are we. The only distinguishing thing that sets us apart is Xclusive's feet, which are a size larger than mine."

The twin on the right then spoke up, saying, "Xtraodinary and I hope that you don't think we are being too forward by approaching you in this manner. We know what it feels like to have total strangers enter your space to comment on your sameness."

The Charles girls are so stunned by the very handsomeness of these bookends that they just stare back at them. For the first time in their lives, neither Catherine nor Cerise said a word.

Chase had to break the ice on this one as her sisters were rendered speechless. Pastor Charles and their mom were obviously amused. The twins were caught, unprepared for this unexpected moment.

"I am Chase Charles, and these are my sisters, Catherine, and Cerise. Those lovely people over there are our parents, Pastor, and Mrs. Charles." Pastor Charles steps over to shake the hands of the young men and to get an understanding of who they are. "Excuse me, young men, but did you say your names are Exclusive and Extraordinary?" the Good Reverend tries hard not to laugh, but the idea of those names had him laughing and fake coughing to cover his amusement.

"It's very nice to meet you, Pastor and Mrs. Charles," he says, with a slight bow to acknowledge them. Continuing, he explains, "We are aware our names aren't exactly conventional ones, but if you have a few minutes to spare, we'd love to enlighten you."

Now intrigued, Pastor Charles speaks, "Please, indulge us," the Good Reverend says. "I'm sure our twins would love to know why your parents would name you as such," he continues, barely containing his laughter.

The Charles twins have no idea how to react to this very uncomfortable situation. They knew the Good Reverend would not be open to allowing his twin princesses to spend one minute with these two Casanovas. The first problem with the "X" twins is that they are too good-looking.

Pastor Charles never liked men he deemed more handsome than a man needed to be.

Xclusive, without hesitation, tells the Charles family that their mother was a single mother raising twin biracial boys. Their father was killed during training exercises at a marine boot camp. Since the twins were without a father, their mother had to work two jobs to support her family. She had the forethought to give her twins names that would give them an edge. She couldn't afford to move them to the best neighbor, so she sought out names that would promote the best in them, both individually and singularly.

Their mother named them "Xclusive without the E and Xtraordinary without the E" to challenge her boys to be confident, intelligent, assertive, and creative. Just as the "X" brothers were about to get into their history, the valets announced the arrival of Charles' family's ride to the airport. Both Catherine and Cerise look at their father with pleading eyes. Pastor Charles knows very well what those looks meant and as usual, he caved in. Not wanting to be the typical father who stands in the way of "whatever this would turn out to be," Pastor Charles invited the "X" twins to join them in the lobby restaurant for lunch. The airport shuttle would have to wait.

During lunch, the "X" twins talked about their lives as doctors and how rewarding their careers are. They were in town for a convention and decided to relax and spend the long weekend at the resort. The young men were high achievers who really loved their mother. They talked incessantly about their commitment to their craft and their plans to further their careers through research.

By the end of lunch, Pastor gave the "X" twins his girl's full names, cell phone numbers, email addresses, and Twitter and Facebook information.

Catherine and Cerise had no objections and looked forward to entertaining the doctors once they all returned home. The "X" twins are currently working in the hospital where the Good Reverend visits the sick and shut-ins from his church.

"What a great freakin' coincidence!" Cerise yelps. The Charles twins are anxious to hear more about the "X" twins as their back story becomes more intriguing by the minute. The Good Reverend would normally shoo away any barflies that looked in the direction of his girls. Chase and Mrs. Charles exchange confused looks. They can't believe whatever just happened there but figured it would all work itself out. Chase hugs her mom and whispers, "Is it just me or is this some kind of weird freak show, side show, prank shit, um, stuff, sorry Mom," she says, forgetting she was speaking to her mom while ducking the head pop she would receive for swearing.

Mrs. Chase couldn't pretend to not find the "X" twins odd, but to be perfectly honest, her twins were far from normal as well. Mrs. Charles and Chase make a move to leave the restaurant, and the rest of the family and the "X" twins follow suit. The group heads toward the exit, where the "X" twins bid the family goodbye. The Charles women are left to swoon over the doctors as the handsome pair walk away. Catherine and Cerise still manage to stay composed until the doctors are out of sight. As soon as the doctors are gone, Cerise pretends to faint into Catherine's arms. The twins hugged and jumped and squealed with delight. They run to their dad and thank him for not embarrassing them too much and getting all up in their business.

The excitement of meeting their "future husbands" would keep the Charles twins in line for a while. Even though the twins were in their 20s, they were still pretty much under the influence of their parents and Chase.

The robbery experience taught Pastor Charles a very important lesson. Meeting the "X" twins was also life-changing event for the Good Reverend. His mind raced with a collection of ideals and thoughts. He steadied himself to carefully compartmentalize his feelings. First lesson, he thought—get professional advice on how to protect their winnings. As soon as they returned home, he would immediately enlist the assistance of an accountant to do estate planning and systematic investments. It wasn't enough to simply spread their winnings around to different banks.

Secondly, Pastor Charles would learn that his first impression of others does not denote who the person really is. He felt ashamed as a man of the cloth and vowed to not repeat this error in judgment again.

Before their visit to the casino resort, the family spent half a year traveling through Europe. Pastor Charles took

The very unexpected cyber robbery gave clarity to the things the Good Reverend took for granted. Protecting his family and his family fortune would become his mantra. Everything else in life would fall way behind those two very important blessings. The Good Reverend wanted to accomplish bigger things in life. His new vision included focusing on goals that would be impactful in society and on a larger scale.

The Charles girls learned some valuable lessons, even though they were totally focused on meeting hot guys and losing their parents in the crowds. They had been so insulated all their lives and were not given enough freedom of how it felt to live the life of a young woman in the real world. Their lives were spent amongst friends and relatives who watched over them always.

Traveling through Europe taught the girls cultural awareness and sensitivity they would never learn at home. The Charles girls were college age, but their limited experience would not allow them to grow and push their limits.

The Charles family stepped over to the valet station as they were alerted of their ride to the airport. Their trip abroad apparently had quite an impact on the girls because they arranged for the family to be picked up in three of the cutest Mini Cooper Convertible cars.

"There must be some mistake," the Good Reverend says, looking confused and annoyed. "No mistake, Daddy. We wanted one last European adventure before going home. Now get in," Cerise orders.

The Good Reverend and Mrs. Charles shrug this one off and hop into the Mini Cooper of their choice. The valets begin to load up the luggage and the Charles girls into their cars. The girls all wave and blow kisses to the valets as the cars speed away.

Mel wandered down to the hotel lobby around 9 pm. She sat down in the most comfortable chair and pulled out her laptop. A waitress darted by from a nearby lounge. Mel flagged the waitress and asked if they served the Diamond Cocktail. The waitress told her it would be a moment and left Mel to adjust in her wonderful place. This is the life Mel always aspired to. The idea that she was in the lobby of the Millionaire Express Casino and Resort, sitting in probably the most comfortable chair in the world, waiting for her cocktail to be delivered was pure heaven. Knowing that the cocktail she ordered is served with a real diamond inside the drink gave her chills. The purchaser of this cocktail had the option to choose the gem of their choice, which would accompany the drink.

The Millionaire Express Casino and Resort was always prepared to accommodate its guests, even with the most outrageous requests, so she knew she would get what she wanted.

After a twenty-minute wait, the waitress reappeared, holding a sterling silver platter. A new, crisp, white napkin was spread over the waitresses' free hand which she, which she placed atop the silver platter. The perfect martini glass was set on the platter, and it was surrounded by four diamond necklaces.

Each necklace held a different stone for the customer to choose from. Mel gazed at each stone, one by one. While sipping her cocktail, Mel slowly lifted each necklace, looking for the perfect cut for herself. She deserves the best, so without hesitation she chooses the one with the most brilliance, most fire and heightened scintillation.

Mel's corporate life placed her in the position of always shopping for "the perfect gift," which helped her become an authority on diamonds, pearls, and colored stones. Mel could sniff out quality with ease.

She placed her black card on the waitresses' silver platter and blindly signed for her forty-three-hundred-dollar martini. Mel casually laid two one-hundred-dollar bills on the tray for the waitress. Her business completed, the waitress abruptly left Mel's presence. Mel turned back to the business waiting for her on her laptop. She just had to finish off the letter she began composing earlier in the day. It read:

Sustaining our friendship will be impossible because we will be separated by great distances. We have shared some of the best times anyone could ever ask for. I really mean that. But now it's time for us all to continue, separately. I want you to grow, to soar. Take chances! Live!

By the way, you will hear some illicit news about how I was involved in the Millionaires Casino robbery. Well, it's true, and I want you to enjoy the extra million you will receive as a bonus. I took the liberty of applying for cyber insurance for each of you in the event your accounts were ever compromised by cyber extraction. The other millionaires will receive the same incentive, so don't feel sorry for them.

Please know this had more to do with applying the skills and training received from the best of the Wall Street gangsters. It has been my pleasure to showcase their effective business practices. Please don't take this personally. It's just business.

It has been my pleasure to work with and for each one of you. Kisses.

Mel hit the send button and headed for the doors. On the way out, she tips the valet guys and waits for her ride.

She enters the back of the limousine, looking refreshed and feeling like a million dollars. Make that an additional 25 million she collected because of the scheme. The extra five million went to the interior guys who worked for the casino. Being in the presence of so much money has a marked effect on the human psyche. Mel's background in human resources proved useful in determining which employees were more likely to take a chance. Mel's instincts were spot on. Her small army of defectors worked with such precision that none of them were considered suspects, nor were they questioned about the cybercrime. Mel had the driver take the slow, scenic route to the airport.

Champagne Life

A private jet was sitting fueled up and ready for Mel's departure. Mel collected her Tumi Alpha cargo bag, neatly and strategically packed with crisp 100.00-dollar bills. As she entered the plane, she had a moment of reflection. This would be her last day on American soil. She contemplated what her life would be like without her family and friends. She would be giving up all the things she worked so hard to attain, but the financial freedom and the ability to take down the corporate clowns she found so very loathsome was worth it.

In that instant, Mel felt light again. She made a mental note to roll around in her millions to keep her spirits up.

Six months into her new life, Mel sits in the middle of her bed surrounded by several fluffy pillows. She's awakened by the crash of the waves in her beautiful villa on a very secluded island.

Every day, she walks down to the island shore to soak up the sun. Mel is tanned and fit from living a more relaxed and leisurely lifestyle. Her biggest decision each day was figuring out what she would eat. Life consisted of days of sitting in the sun, meditating, exploring the island and collecting shells. On occasion, Mel would dip into town to purchase food and supplies.

She befriended a local farmer named Nicholas, who made certain Mel had everything she needed. For his attentiveness, Mel rewards Nicholas handsomely. She would pay double for everything Nicholas brought to her. Nicholas didn't feel right taking the extra money from "Ms. Mel," as he referred to her, but Mel insisted. Even if Nicholas tried returning the overpayments, he would always find an envelope filled with cash in his mailbox. After a long while, Nicholas just gave up.

The extra cash was more than Nicholas needed for his simple life, so he opened a separate account to store the extra funds. That separate bank account would become Mel's downfall.

Almost a year to the day, Mel would receive a visit from men in dark suits. Mel let the detectives in and offered them refreshments. The detectives explained to Mel that they were there to place her under arrest for various crimes related to the Millionaires Express Casino and Resort.

A broad smile came across Mel's face as the detectives rattled on about her Miranda rights and the charges.

In the process of placing handcuffs on Mel, she warned and assured the men in dark suits that her villa is wired with a very intricate set of explosives. Her detailed knowledge of the type of explosives within the walls of her villa left the detectives uneasy, but they called her bluff.

Mel quickly pressed the detonator inside the hoodie of her jacket and that set off a powerful explosion at the back of her villa. The explosion blew out the back porch and laundry area of Mel's villa. She looks at the detectives without blinking and announces, "I have nothing to lose by blowing up the rest of this motherfucker. I can do it with or without. Your choice."

The detectives were quite stunned by this revelation but cautiously backed out of the villa, vowing to return. That explosion was powerful, and apparently this lady is dangerous and deadly.

If the detectives had done their homework, they would have known that Mel is well connected and stays ready. She immediately finds a source for whatever is needed when she needs something. Pyrotechnic experts were used for a New Year's celebration at a company function. The average person has no use for a pyrotechnic expert, but Mel is not your average Joe. She was paid to come up with new ideas to keep the staff fully engaged while making her bosses look generous, innovative and miles ahead of the competition. The Penthouse Suites were known for hiring the smartest and most talented executives, and the top brass always took credit for bringing them onboard. The fireworks display was an example of the little something extra to show the staff and their families' appreciation. Mel made that happen.

Thinking out of the box is a skill set for Mel. It's how she lives her life and the reason she is successful. She has to always think of all the possibilities, and she rarely sleeps.

If law enforcement wasn't so damn thirsty to track her halfway around the globe, she would never have had to set off the explosives. This is how Mel rationalized the whole experience. The fact that she and her accomplices ripped off a bunch of innocent people, as well as the casino, was rationalized as a "Robinhood" experience. Her rationalization of the explosives is that it was "mere theatrics." She would never kill anyone. The looks on the detectives' faces were priceless.

When law enforcement returned with backup, they found the villa empty, and Mel long gone. The federal agents questioned the locals about Mel's whereabouts, but no one had seen her all week. After scouting the island and coming up empty, the federal agents and Constable left the island.

Mel hadn't clearly planned out what she would do if caught. The very thought of being caught never entered her mind. She was so very careful with her movements thereafter, and kept close tabs of the news back in the states. She laid low at a neighboring hotel and island resort. She would only leave her room when necessary. Mel was a survivor, but she was in unchartered waters. She had never been on the wrong side of the law. She had never even received a traffic ticket. Survival instincts alone would not do. She had to take care of herself, with the notion that she would never be caught, period.

Mel figured there would be pictures of her circulated around the various islands, so her new mission was to settle into the new island but do so with her guard up. That very night, Old Mel vanished out of her haven and disappeared off the island. New Mel never left her suite without a wig, a hat, sunglasses, or a combination of them all.

The hotel resort was a beautiful oasis in the middle of an island that had little to offer its natives. Most of the workers made little to nothing, judging from their after-hours attire. The locals jammed the rickety hot buses after work, which took them home every evening.

One thing Mel knew for sure were people. She knew that most people wanted a better life for themselves and their families. Hell, that's how she ended up in this predicament.

Mel began studying the hotel workers as they came and went to her suite. The room service staff was eager to please, and Mel did not hold back on gratuities.

Sometimes, late at night, Mel would slink down to the restaurant for a bite and to get some fresh air. She was careful to always cover up without looking too out of place. There were many Americans on the islands, so she tried to blend in and not draw attention to herself.

The flyer that was circulating described Mel from her pre-heist existence. Mel was able to create different versions of herself at a moment's notice. No one suspected she was the woman the foreign police were inquiring about. Mel also learned the natives were weary of government officials, law enforcement, the visiting clergy, and something called Laars of the Cave.

Apparently, Laars from the Cave used bats to scope out and kidnap the villagers while they slept.

Mel was careful not to flaunt her money around the locals, but she had to always keep a stash on her, just in case. She played the island like any other tourist.

Before long, she befriended two fishermen she had been studying for a while. Mel noted that these fishermen were islanders and not commuting from the mainland. The fishermen worked hard from sunup till sundown. They would set up their nets and wait for the fish to contact the bait. After about thirty minutes, the fishermen would reel in their catch and load up their boat. This continued for about four straight hours until their catch boat was full. At about noon, the fishermen would sell off their catch to local buyers.

For one full week, Mel would purchase the catch from the two fishermen at double the going rates than the wholesale buyers. She would then give the fish to the hotel workers to bring home to their families. The fishermen were suspicious of Mel's motives at first, but when they learned she was feeding the locals with the fish she purchased from them, they would soon accept her as a friend of the village.

During the end of the second week of Mel's time with her fishermen friends, Mel was seated on the dock, sharing the case of Heineken she purchased for everyone. The fishermen, their wives, and a few children were singing a native song about their homeland. Mel sat among them as she helped the women clean the fish and ready them for sale. Mel was touched by their acceptance of her and grateful for the camaraderie.

In the distance, the group spotted an official government speed boat, headed their way.

There appeared to be six officers on board. A smaller boat followed closely behind the main one. Mel looked deep into the eyes of her comrades. Without hesitation, one of the two fishermen whistled loudly in the direction of the tub. The tub was the catch boat that held the catch of the day. It was pulled around to where Mel was sitting.

There wasn't much time, but everyone knew what they had to do. The women quickly began to fill the tub with the catch until the bottom of the tub was full. Mel gave Nicholas the stash of cash inside her Louis Vuitton fanny pack. She wanted Nicholas to have the fanny pack as it would fetch a hefty sum for him, but he insisted she keep it. She had done so much for the villagers that he did not want to take advantage of it. Besides, fishermen in those parts had no business with that kind of extravagance. The law would figure he stole it from a tourist and would bring him up on charges. He quickly thanked Mel for everything.

The fishermen and their wives quickly began to fill the tub before coaxing Mel to get in with the catch. Mel looked out at the crew and stared into the faces of the people that would help her escape. Her eyes were full of tears. She wasn't frightened by the prospect of being caught.

Mel was so full of admiration and respect for the people whom she knew so little about, but they showed her a loyalty she would never find before. Before the group covered Mel's face with the smelly fish of the sea, Mel removed her diamond necklace and placed it in the hand of Nicholas' wife, Zita. Zita grinned broadly, then blew a kiss to Mel, just as the last fish covered Mel's face. The group continued filling the tub until it was almost full.

The coast guard boats reached the dock as the tub was being prepped for launch.

The officers immediately jumped onto the pier and dispersed in all directions. The officials began questioning the locals, flashing pictures of Mel. The fishermen and their wives looked perplexed and began speaking to each other in their native tongue.

The officers resorted to sign language as none of the officers spoke the dialect of the villagers and were unable to communicate with them. The officers then held the pictures of Mel close to the group, but none of them recognized the woman in the pictures.

The tub boat began to pull away from the shore when the officer in charge ordered it to stop. The air and everything on earth that moved came to a screeching halt. The head officer ordered two of the officers to search the tub boat. The officers begrudgingly began unloading the tub boat, throwing the fish back into the sea. They unloaded the tub boat to the horror and dismay of the fishermen. When half the tub boat had been emptied out, one of the officials yelled, "All right, that's enough. There's nothing there! Let's go!"

The two officers then jump out of the tub boat and back onto shore. The official then gives the tub boat captain the go-ahead to leave. The tub boat pulls away, heading toward the horizon. The officials board their boat and then head back in the direction from which they came.

When the official boat was clearly out of sight, the fishermen, their wives, and children broke out into laughter. They were so excited and happy for Mel. They break open the remaining Heinekens and raise them to Mel. Their shouts of "Mel!Mel!Mel!" in honor of their friend by the sea echoed in the winds of the tiny island.

Mel's tub boat was a tiny speck in the vast sea as the sun began to set. For the first time in a very long time, Mel could taste the salty tears she wept during this unceremonious departure.

The night air and dulcet tones of Ratay, the tugboat captain, lulled her to sleep.

Mel awakened to the smell of fish and ocean air. She was utterly confused, not knowing how long she'd slept nor how far Ratay had taken her. Ratay was careful to stay away from the shore. He was given strict orders to keep Mel safe.

No one was allowed to come within a mile of the tugboat, and Ratay was to deliver Mel to Hollow Isle, undetected. The natives knew the sea and the surrounding shore better than anyone, so the mission was both clear and easy.

As she sat up, Mel felt delirious, seasick, and very hungry. She steadied herself and slowly began peeling away the catch from under her arms, thighs and hair. She began to analyze all that she had done. "Was it worth all of this?" Mel asked herself. "Did I do the right thing?" These thoughts flooded Mel's foggy mind.

By the time Mel and Ratay reached the shore, her ruminations were quite clear. "Hell yeah, it was worth it!" she yells as Ratay pulls up to her island. This new island was more beautiful than the last. Mel tried to make herself as presentable as she could for someone who spent unmeasured time on a fisherman's tugboat. She thanked Ratay profusely and paid him $5,000 for the ride. Ratay tried to give the money back, but Mel wouldn't hear of it. Cash was something Mel knows all about. She knows its power and the influence it has on people. Those cash payouts bought her the loyalty she needed from the people she so desperately needed. Ratay took off, heading home. Mel waved with delight from the shore. Her next adventure was a few footsteps away.

The sun was setting on the beach resort, which looked like another tropical paradise. The resort was surrounded by mile high-palm trees. There were white wicker rockers along the landing. Bird of paradise plants stood neatly between the palm trees, while potted ferns hung high from the ceiling above. The gentle breeze made everything all right as Mel made her way to the next adventure which would include enough food to feed a party of five.

Within half an hour of her arrival, Mel was sitting in a hot tub, devouring the biggest lobster tail she'd ever seen and sipping champagne. When she finally came up for air and her appetite had settled down, she began to look at her surroundings with amazement and sheer joy. From her tub, she could see the bed she would soon lay her head on. She imagined the thread count was somewhere beyond, beyond. She noticed her sitting area had a 75-inch plasma television, a fully stocked bar, and there was a private jacuzzi on the veranda. After a series of champagne burps, Mel blurts out, "Damn straight it was worth it!"

Morning came with a freshness that could only be described as a honey-hued ray of beauty. Mel was up before sunrise. She was anxious, but not in a bad way. She was anxious to see the sunrise from her new setting. Mel was so thankful the Federale pulled out when they did, as her life on the run allowed her to explore life from a perspective most people can't imagine.

Once the sun displayed its full beauty, it suddenly dawned on her that she had no idea where she was. She arrived nauseated, disoriented, and afraid. A minor detail like where she was, had not occurred to her. Ratay didn't tell her where she was going. Her friends on shore were familiar with the neighboring islands and were only concerned with sending her where she would be safe.

Mel was hesitant to venture out on the veranda as she had not had a chance to check out her surroundings. There were heavy blackout drapes, but suddenly closing them on such a beautiful morning might draw some unwanted attention to her room. For now, it would be better to keep the drapes open but play it safe.

She sat at the lovely Victorian desk and decided to map out her next move. She began the strategic process of moving her funds around. Her vast knowledge of the private banking world and her many connections taught her when to invest, where to place large sums, undetected, and how to access those funds at a moment's notice. Mel held the secrets of some very prominent individuals over the years. Those individuals were happy to assist Mel in any way possible. As long as she held their confidence, they would provide her with whatever she needed to remain undetected and below the radar.

Before long, she has access to her money, a new passport and new identity, a travel visa, and the phone numbers of individuals that may be able to help her if she needs them.

Her next moves were much easier as they required her knowledge of top-level service. She summoned the hotel concierge to her room, and three hours later, a new computer printer arrived, along with several clothing options, all carefully purchased from the hotel boutique. She also received a collection of beautiful sunglasses, hats, and scarves. Mel's knowledge of top-level service always served her well. The concierge left her room with a big smile and an even bigger tip.

Mel waited a few moments before she responded to an unexpected knock at her suite door. "Mademoiselle, it is Fatimah from the salon," the voice whispered. "Leo sent me to assist you," she continued. Mel cautiously opens the door to let Fatimah in. Not one to be caught sleeping, Mel begins questioning Fatimah about herself. It was important to get details of the people that came into her space. She would later question them about the information garnered through these social exchanges. Before allowing Fatimah to begin the tedious process of transforming her tresses, Mel grilled the woman about her life to see if she could trip her up. When she was certain Leo hadn't double crossed her and Fatimah hadn't turned out to be some asshole official, Fatimah was allowed to get to work.

Fatimah was an exceptional and polished beautician and aesthetician. By the time she finished, she had transformed Mel into a platinum blonde empress. Mel was super impressed with Fatimah's skills. Before she left, Mel handed Fatimah twenty-one-hundred-dollar bills. Fatimah tried to let Mel know the service was only three hundred dollars. Mel gently placed the money in Fatimah's hands and assured her that the money was hers indeed. She also mentioned that she was a very private person and she expected Fatimah would not speak about their meeting, nor would she ever mention how she transformed Mel's looks. Mel then tipped Fatimah another thousand dollars and gave her some of the clothing from the hotel's boutique. Mel knows silence is golden, but she also knows it is green. Fatimah slipped out of Mel's room and never uttered a word about their encounter.

Mel stared at her reflection in the bathroom for a very long time. She never had an issue with her looks before, but the person looking back at her intimidated her. The reflection held beauty she had never seen before, but the reflection also had her experiencing huge deformations of the monstrous sort. Her mind was playing tricks on her and her consciousness was now a bitch named Karma. Karma was not going to allow Mel to enjoy this beautiful transformation. Mel was well versed in psychological mind games, psychotherapy, and physiological psychology.

She'd learned that the mind can only handle so much information at a time, and at this very moment, it was very focused on the sexy woman in front of her. The person staring back at Mel was freakishly beautiful, with hair now the color of a mythical Greek Goddess, skin turned bronze from her days in the sun, and she was now a couple sizes smaller than she had been in years. The clothes, hand selected by the concierge, fit like a glove. Today, she wore a tan suit that compliments her body so much so, it looked like it was poured on. The pants were slightly bell-bottomed with a cuff, and the jacket was a two-button tailored sort. He had also purchased a pair of sunglasses with a rich blue tint and a pair of killer sandals with four-inch heels. The pants covered most of the shoes, gave her the appearance of a rising star.

The longer Mel studied the woman in the mirror, the more uncomfortable she became with herself. After a while, she gave whoever the woman was, staring back at her in the mirror the middle finger, then walked out of her hotel suite.

As she turned the corner to take the elevator, Mel noticed two men in dark suits approaching. Her mind raced with thoughts of what to do. She could feel herself hyperventilating, shaking, and slowly fading.

When Mel came to, the men whom she feared were helping her to her feet. She then realized she panicked for no reason at all. As the men helped her up, she realized how very handsome they both were. One of them even looked like her former lover, and he smelled really good.

Mel thanked the gentlemen for their kindness and assured them she was just tired from her long flight with little sleep. The men bade her farewell and entered the elevator. Mel quickly returned to her hotel suite, packed her belongings, and before long, she was on a plane destined for Bali. Mel always had a fascination with the Mulia Resort in Nusa, Dua, Indonesia. During her university years, a group of friends decided to take a trip abroad for a fun-filled spring break.

That vacation stayed with Mel, and it would become her new destination. From what she could remember, the resort was everything. It provided beauty, privacy, warm beaches, endless days of sunlight, great food, and wonderful service.

The island also provided its guests a haven for recuperating plastic surgery patients without being noticed or hounded by the paparazzi. It was just the type of privacy Mel needed now.

As the flight touched down, Mel gathered her belongings and began the walk down the jet way. Suddenly, an uneasy, overwhelming feeling came over her. To calm herself, she began doing breathing exercises to release the anxiety that had somehow taken over. This was outside her normal range of emotions. Fear was never something that consumed Mel in this way.

Switching reels, she begins to troubleshoot the issue consuming her thoughts as well as her physical being. A tactic she used to calm herself when overwhelmed was counting. She would count her steps everywhere she went to combat her overly active mind. By counting her steps, her brain would be consumed with the idea of not losing count, and that would stop her from having panic attacks. Mel immediately recognized what was happening, and the self-check exercises slowed her pulse, re-set the sweat glands, and controlled her breathing pattern. She was going to be okay.

That was until she exited the jet way. No sooner than she stepped into the airport, she was immediately triggered by the sight of six Indonesian officers waiting and looking in her direction. "Well, I guess the jig is up," Mel thought to herself. She slowly placed her bag onto the airport floor, and stood helpless, almost lifeless, waiting for her fate.

As the officers approached her, Mel never looked up, never flinched. She waited for them to read her rights. A single droplet of sweat managed to escape her sweat glands, emanating at the base of her neck, and slowly rolling down the center of her back, finally resting at the tip of her French cut, lace thong.

The six officers brushed past Mel, almost shoving her to the side as they gave a hearty welcome to their sons, the winning little league baseball team that were on Mel's flight. By the time the little leaguers and the officers were heading for baggage claim, Mel was a puddle of sweat and pee. She camped out in the airport lounge for the next four hours.

Mel could hear the hum of the air conditioning unit as she entered her suite. Instead of a group of college-aged girls running and screaming, calling dibs on which bed they wanted, Mel graciously enters the suite, followed by a bellhop and room service. On her way up to her room, she phoned in her dinner, and as a starter, ordered a carafe of vodka martinis, chilled toward freezing, jalapeno-filled olives, and a slew of M&Ms. These were Mel's comfort foods, and right now she needed lots of comfort. Her plan was to eat, take a hot shower and then go to bed. The whole airport experience had wiped her out, well that and the four vodka martinis she swished down at the airport to calm herself down.

After a great meal and she had fully showered, Mel slipped into bed. Before turning out the lights, she happened to glance at herself in the full-length mirror on the wall. Her transformation was quite stunning. She no longer resembled the old Mel. *New Mel was much more interesting to look at,* she thought. She then slid under the covers and fell asleep.

The next morning, Mel was awakened by the smell of hot pancakes, eggs, piping hot coffee, fresh fruit, and, of course, an ice bucket filled with icy champagne. She was still groggy from the night before, so was slow to recognize that she'd pre-ordered all this the night before. As she rolls over, she comes face-to-face with a small man in a white waiter's coat and a big smile.

Mel didn't immediately react to the stranger but instantly went into protective mode. The urge to fight was always at the forefront of Mel's thoughts, particularly after yesterday's fiasco, but she waited. She waited until her vision was clear, along with her head and her heartbeat. She then slowly reached for the nearest, hardest, throwable thing she could find—the lamp.

When the small man realized Mel was about to clock him, he held up both hands and began backing away. This sign of retreat was a little confusing, but Mel couldn't take any chances. "Why are you here?" Mel asked. Her body language made it quite clear she would not hesitate to brain the small man with the lamp. "I am here to serve you, ma'am," the man responded. His voice was that of a well-spoken Englishman with the expert training taught by the finest butler's schools in all of England. "Who sent you?" Mel asks, still guarded and unwilling to put down the lamp held above her head. "You ordered me when you arranged for your suite ma'am," the man replied. "I will be your houseman for as long as you're here. I'm here to set up your breakfast, which will consist of buttered toast, scrambled eggs, pancakes with American syrup, fresh fruit, and icy cold champagne. I also have a side order of M&Ms and jalapeno stuffed olives for you."

Mel glares at the small man while he gestures to show her the pamphlet. She allows him to place the pamphlet on the bedside table. With catlike precision, Mel leaps from the bed and picks up the pamphlet, which details the features that come with the suite. A quick glance over the room details proves that the small is authentic. Before Mel can apologize for her actions, the man is busying himself arranging the food on the plate. He continues the breakfast set up with a pour of the icy champagne into her crystal flute. Finally, he pulls out her chair for her to sit in, all the while bowing a servant's bow, white napkin draped over his arm. Mel, now thoroughly embarrassed, acquiesced and moved to the table to eat. The small man gently takes the lamp from Mel's hand as he spreads her napkin onto her lap.

After devouring her breakfast, Mel excused herself and went into the bathroom. Once inside, she began laughing hysterically to herself. She was more than familiar with the top-shelf handling of clients as the Suites were known for their world-famous "high lifestyle clientele." Mel was used to setting up these types of arrangements for others but was never on the receiving end of this treatment.

After what seemed like a very long time, Mel finally exits the bathroom, fully refreshed and ready to start her day. The small man had already cleared the table and put everything away, except for a fresh glass of icy champagne. He hands her the sparkling beverage and continues clearing away the dishes. He had already made her bed, opened the drapes and turned on the local news station for her.

Mel cleared her throat, attempting to address the small man, when he matter-of-factly said, "Joseph, ma'am, my name is Joseph." Mel takes a moment before responding. "Well, um, Joseph, I just want to apologize for my behavior earlier. It's just that you startled me and I…I wasn't expecting to have you here. I hope you understand," she finishes.

"No need to apologize, ma'am, you're not the first armed guest to accost me while fulfilling my duties. I must say, you Americans have quite the dramatic flair and are the most combat-ready guests I have come across."

Mel didn't know if this was a dig toward Americans or not but decided to let it go since she was just inches away from laying him out only a few minutes earlier.

The day was ticking away, so Mel decided to start getting ready and set about unpacking and settling in. She began strolling around the suite, searching for her bags. "Your belongings are unpacked and in your dressing room," Joseph announces without looking up. Mel meekly heads in the wrong direction to what she believed was her dressing room. "The other way," Joseph says without so much as a glance. Mel quickly changes direction and heads toward her dressing room. Once inside she is floored by Joseph's attention to detail. Her clothes were perfectly hung in color-coordinated fashion. All shoes were lined up along a lighted shoe display area, and the walls were covered in floor-to-ceiling lighted mirrors. A long black velvet bench stretched the length of the dressing room, and next to it, a small round table with a bucket of icy cold champagne and another crystal flute. Mel grinned a devilish grin and began selecting an outfit for the day.

Joseph stood in the doorway at attention, waiting for Mel as she exited her dressing room.

She did a quick spin around for Joseph's blessing. Joseph gave a slight bow, indicating his approval of her wardrobe selection. "Will there be anything else Ma'am," Joseph asks.

"Thank you, Joseph, that will be all," Mel responds. "I left the lunch menu on your jardinière, Ma'am. Your day maid will arrive shortly to tend to your suite." Mel stood smiling politely and blinking, not knowing what else to say or do. Joseph responded with a short bow and closed the door to the suite. Mel stood silent for a moment, wondering why she would need a day maid for a suite that was already close to perfect.

Shortly after Joseph's departure, Mel leaves her suite. She sashays down the hotel hallway in a two-piece jumpsuit and coat combination. The powder blue ensemble is flawless and very complimentary of Mel's physique. Mel feels good and is enjoying the attention she receives from both men and women. Old Mel always felt she had a small audience of admirers that thought she was pretty, but the new Mel, with her new style, better than ever physique, and awesome hair color, gave her another level of attention she had never known.

Mel also enjoyed the freedom of being anonymous, glamorous, and rich. Yes, she had to live underground, but having endless funds made life that much easier. Living life on the edge also gave her LIFE! Life like she'd never experienced it before. She had no idea what she would do today; she only knew she would be happy. Her encounter with Joseph shook her up quite a bit, but she knew she would not live her life with that level of fear again. After all, she thought, no one knows who I am, and no one can possibly recognize me. I barely recognize myself. The more she thought about it, the more at ease she felt. With that resolve, Mel decides to cozy up to the hotel bar and order the house special. She had no idea what the house special was, but when it arrived, Mel laughed and clapped with glee. The waiter brought over a huge ceramic bowl, shaped like a seashell, filled to the rim, completely in flames. The fire would indicate the drink was heavily fueled. Mel blew out the fire and began drinking the tasty treat until it was gone.

It wasn't until after the drink was gone that the waiter shared the fact that the drink was traditionally made for two. A now glassy-eyed Mel could only burp and hiccup.

A group of tourists entered the bar and plopped down across from where Mel was seated.

She glanced at the group through her dark shades, studying their behavior and admiring their camaraderie. Before long, the bar began to fill up with locals and tourists alike. Mel looked around and vicariously enjoyed the spirit, laughter, and excitement the crowd drew from each other. Mel sat and people watched for another couple of hours, then slowly made her way back to her room. She decided she would venture out later.

Six months into her new arrangement, Mel had become restless. Remembering that her restlessness is what brought her to today, she backed out of a conversation with her inner voice and settled herself. She also remembered that the same feeling of restlessness is what drove her into the arms of Max. That feeling was an internal battle she knew she must shake, but something inside her would not allow her to. Mel always thought she should have done better things in her life. The drive was always there, but the opportunities never were. No matter how happy she believed she was, she always thought there was more. Whatever the "more" was, it had eluded her. "Is it time to move on?" she thought. This thought stayed with her for days on end.

One evening, Mel found herself speaking out loud, "Why am I never satisfied?"

"It seems you can have anything you want," Joseph replies. Mel was startled by Joseph's response, as she had forgotten he was preparing her tea tray as she settled in for the evening. "I used to want all of the things I now have, but …" her voice trailing off. She stops short of complaining, recognizing she was living in a four-thousand-dollars-a-night suite, complete with a butler and day maid.

"Perhaps you need to face whatever the disappointment or heartache that has devastated you," Joseph asserts.

"That's quite insightful of you, Joseph, but I am neither disappointed nor heartbroken, thank you, Joseph," she curtly snaps.

"I am deeply sorry for overstepping, Ma'am, and I sincerely apologize."

"No apologies needed, Joseph, you're probably right," she confessed. "There are some things left unsaid and undone in my life. But I certainly don't want to burden you with my ramblings."

"Okay, then Ma'am. I guess you're all good here then?" Joseph asks, backing out with his cart.

"We're all good, Joseph." She smiles. "And Joseph," she continues, "I am very sorry for snapping at you."

"Apology accepted, Ma'am," Joseph says with a little smile and a quick bow. "May I offer you any further assistance this evening, Ma'am?"

"Thank you, Joseph. You've been a godsend. That will be all." Joseph takes his tray and exits the suite for the evening.

The next morning Joseph enters Mel's suite and begins his daily regimen of preparing her breakfast, preparing her restroom and dressing room to help her begin her day. After last night's talk, Joseph decided a hearty meal would be just what the doctor ordered. After a good meal and a long hot bath, an icy cold glass of champagne, little Missy would be okay. Joseph is excited about the prospect of making Mel feel good about herself. He prepares a meal fit for a queen. When the meal preparation was done, he slowly turned up the island music Miss enjoys and electronically pulled back the drapes to awaken her slowly. The aroma of the island coffee filled the air to ignite her senses, and the sweet scent of the fresh gardenias awaited her as well.

Joseph then stands at attention, waiting for Missy to awaken from her slumber. He waited for almost an hour before gently clearing his throat, trying to get her attention. Against his better judgment, Joseph went to turn on the night light next to Mel's bed. He is both shocked and confused by what he finds. He looked more closely at the bed, then pulled back the covers; he was shocked to see no one there. He went to her dressing room and knocked. No answer there either. He hesitantly went to the bathroom and knocked. He called out her name before entering. No one there either. Joseph even searched out on the veranda. Mel was not there.

A sudden wave of sadness comes over Joseph. He thought he'd failed as a personal valet in satisfying his client to the fullest. He felt inadequate and ashamed. He sits quietly at the foot of Missy's bed and contemplates his fate. Surely the company would let him go. After a while, he slowly begins the process of pulling the room back together for the next guests. He had to prepare the room for re-assignment. As he begins gathering the plates from his beautifully prepared breakfast, he notices an envelope on the butler's pantry. Joseph picked up the envelope that bore his name. He eagerly opens the envelope and reads the note inside. A huge sigh of relief comes over him as he imagines Missy must have gone for a stroll and would surely be returning soon. He holds the note to his chest before reading it again.

Dearest Joseph,

I want to thank you for your warm spirit, your kind, gentle ways, but most of all, your wisdom. You've taught me so much during our time together. I wish I'd met you years ago so you could have taught me what's important in life. I had it all wrong, Joseph. I can't thank you enough for setting me straight. I left something on the nightstand for you and your daughter.

Please use it to enhance your lives. You deserve this and much, much more. Take care.

Missy.

Joseph slowly walks toward the nightstand and opens the drawer. After a few ticks, he comes across the sealed envelope and finds it filled, stuffed, with one-hundred-dollar bills. Joseph concludes the envelope holds thousands of dollars. He sits on the side of the bed and begins to weep like a small child. No one had ever rewarded Joseph with such immense kindness.

When the suite was totally clean and ready for re-assignment, Joseph escorts the day maids out and hands them a handsome tip for their work. Joseph smiles a heartfelt-filled smile, then turns out the lights and shuts the door to Missy's suite.

Mel's obsession with money continues to drive her in ways she will never understand. She hates the idea that there is such an uneven distribution of wealth in the world, yet she is totally enamored with the idea of living well. She knows she is a walking breathing contradiction of herself because living life without limits, remarkable fashion, tasteful jewelry, and on and on and on, gives her the biggest rush of dopamine. It is an endless cycle for her, and she knows it is the "thing", the driving force, that turns her pages.

She believes everyone should have the opportunity to live life with limitless possibilities. She grapples with the idea of world wealth. How can she help as many people as she can experience this feeling? The very thought of it all tingles her insides.

One day, while wandering around the very small village of Dhoker Jhara in Jharkland, Mel found herself in that indeterminable place called "the middle of nowhere." She had no idea where she was exactly, but she was drawn to the area because of its raw beauty. At the center of the small village stood a single building with the name scrawled across it on a wooden board. She couldn't quite make out the name, but her curious nature got the best of her. She walks right up to the front door and heads inside. As she walks the halls of each floor of the building, she is astonished to see children of all ages so engaged in the learning process. She is even more intrigued that they are all gathered around their teacher, sharing one book for each classroom. The children hold a striking resemblance to one another.

Mel later learns that a small colony of nomads had settled in the tiny village. They are a peaceful group that work the land and grow their own food. They took care of their families and lived a peaceful existence until a group of militias came along and practically wiped out a whole generation. The people of the village worked hard to reestablish themselves. They built the school themselves, vowing to ensure a better life for the generations to come. Never had she seen people who were genuinely dedicated to educating their youth. Mel knew she had to somehow help the process and use her money for good.

The very idea of doing something that benefited so many gave her a lift she never imagined. Mel rushed back to her new hotel room and began planning. Within weeks of her stumbling across the school, Mel starts the process to ensure the village receives whatever is needed to succeed.

Mel's stay in Jharkland didn't last long. On her way to the next stop, she asks her driver to stop by the village to see the progress. By the time she reached the school, the trucks were already there, unloading clothing, shoes, backpacks, food, and trinkets for every kid in the school. The administrators, teachers, and children alike were all confused by the large trucks that arrived, carrying so many wonderful things for the children. The instructions were translated by one of the elders. Each child was to receive one of everything. Mel was careful to not contribute to starting a society of haves and have-nots. Everyone was to receive it all.

Her next stop was a trip to the farmlands, a few miles up the road. Mel learned that the farmers had to borrow money to even purchase the seeds for their crops. By the time the harvest was due, the payout for the crops was more than the farmers anticipated, so the cycle of poverty was an endless one.

Mel organized a group of conservationists to visit the farms and farmers to teach them how to operate a very simple irrigation system. The farmers could then maintain their crops and bring in a harvest that allowed them to feed their families and turn a profit. The idea that she was helping this village of people become self-sufficient again turned Mel completely on.

On the eighth day of the eighth month of that year, Mel was becoming increasingly more restless. Her restlessness did not come from a place of her past desires but from her need to set things right in the world. She isn't naive enough to believe she is some sort of superhero, but she knows what humans are capable of, if given a chance. Mel is slowly becoming somewhat of a champion for the underdogs of the world.

Some of the poorest regions throughout the world began receiving shipments of various and unique gifts. These gifts came in the form of self-help machinery, medical supplies, seeds for start-up gardens, pop-up tents filled with a hefty supply of laptops, cellphones, electronic books, and transportation vehicles. Every region had been carefully researched to ensure they received the assistance that promoted growth and education.

Mel is the happiest she has been in a long time. Maybe ever. Her philanthropic efforts were being talked about around the globe. She loves the idea that no one knows who this "Philanthropic Heiress" is, and she also gets a kick out of them naming her as such. Mellowed that she is fighting poverty, illness, and helping to educate those who would not ordinarily become educated, Mel flourishes in the knowledge that she can change lives. Joseph would be so proud of me, she thinks. Her happiness no longer depends on how well she is living, but how well others are living. The external circumstance that catapulted her life (along with the extra boost from her fellow millionaires) is not a fleeting sensation for her. Once Mel became aware of what was happening to her, she suddenly realized her goal post of wealth was moving in another direction. She is no longer interested in ways to seek out a bigger fortune for herself. Pursuing material wealth and comparing her life to those she deems better off than she is no longer relevant. That thought process is what led her to her unfulfilled life. The restlessness she fought so hard to contain came from her own ambitions to overcome her sense of herself. The next best thing would always be beyond her reach because the next best thing was ever changing.

The social circles she so desperately sought to infiltrate were a distant memory. Mel had finally come into her own, and she wanted to celebrate that victory. The only problem now is that she is distant from everything and everyone she thought added meaning to her life. This is the very moment Mel comes to terms with how very screwed up she had been all those years. Through self-healing and becoming aware of what life is truly about, she realizes what a totally jacked up individual she is.

Those feelings washed over her like a tidal wave. She suddenly fell ill with the pain of heartache and sorrow like never before. The realization that she could have been happy in her life with the level of joy she was already a party to, practically suffocates her. Her life before this journey would have fulfilled most people, but she always thought it wasn't enough. Her friends and co-workers respected her for the woman she was. Her family loved her for who she was. John loved her for who she was. The nagging restlessness got the best of her, in the worst way.

Many months passed before Mel made her next move. A new force was pulling her in a different direction. She had been contemplating this move for a while but opted to put it out of her mind. This move would be the riskiest of all, but she has to somehow find her way back home. She has no idea of what home means anymore, but she is tired of running. Many years had passed, and life for everyone had moved on, everyone but her.

Though she had grown in ways she never dreamed of, she desperately wanted to share her new life with the people that meant something to her. She wants the people that love her to know that she no longer values those things in life, but life itself.

Mel contemplated her reentry into society for days on end. But what would she say to everyone? What, if anything, would anyone say to her? Would they be happy, knowing she is still alive, or would they immediately call the authorities on her? Prison was one thing Mel was not going to do. She had already rationalized she would not make a model prisoner, so that was out. She had to devise a plan to get back into the world while figuring out how not to go to jail. That made her wonder if there was a reward out for her arrest. She mulled over all the thoughts, both positive and negative. The old Mel was a savvy, driven businesswoman. The old Mel would not let anything stand in her way of getting what she wanted. The old Mel would look for and find the loophole that would keep her from becoming someone's bitch in prison.

Mel sat inside the airport lounge preparing her defense to reclaim her life. She decided to go to Athens, where she could relax and enjoy the luxe life, she'd grown accustomed to. No sense in living a dull life just because you're an international fugitive. She fully understood the intoxicating lifestyles of the very rich. It was everything she thought it would be, and more. Giving it all up would be a heavy sacrifice. Mel knew that to live again, she would have to die. Not die in the physical sense, but she would have to kill off the demons that wealth and power held over her.

As Mel enters her suite at the Athens Towers, she is thoroughly exhausted. She spent the entire flight fighting with herself. The long flight left her anxious and very hungry. After settling in, she walks down to the main dining room to eat and try to relax. She looks around to find the most secluded, darkest table, something she did without a thought. She'd become accustomed to dining alone and keeping a low profile. Tonight, would be no different.

The meal was superb. Mel ate every bit of the moussaka. She asked the server for the exotic Greek dish, hoping it was as good as the last time she was there. She also ordered a bottle of champagne to wash it all down and help her relax. "Old habits die hard," she thought as she slowly makes her way back to her suite. She dipped into the gift shop in the lobby to pick up a few things when suddenly a voice from somewhere in the store yelled out "Mel! Mel is that you?" the voice continues. Her instincts told her not to react, but to ignore the person calling out. She doesn't turn around, breathe, nor blink, nor move a muscle. She doesn't react in any way.

The voice of the man who thought he knew the platinum blonde woman must have realized it wasn't the person he thought it was and he left the store. Mel waited a full ten minutes before turning around. When she finally turns around, she sees that there was no one in the gift store but the store clerk and herself. She quickly gathers the items she's purchasing and hurriedly places them on the counter.

This was the reality check she needed. "How in the hell did that idiot, whoever he was, figure out who she was?"

The store clerk has been watching the whole ordeal with amusement. "Guess you really didn't want to talk to the old boy, huh?" Startled by the clerk's sassiness, Mel responds guardedly. "Um, yes, I wasn't trying to be rude, I'm just tired from the long flight."

"Oh, I get it!" the clerk continues as he rings up Mel's purchases. "Some people don't know when to give it a rest," he continues, shaking his head as if he and Mel share the same secret. "That guy was checking you out from the moment you walked in. I like the way you played him off. That was real gangsta!" Mel stands stoically, staring at the store clerk for a moment, then decides he is gross, and she needs to get away from him too. She quickly pays for her things and then gases it out of there.

By the time she reaches her room, she is shaking like a leaf. Someone recognized her, even with the new trim figure, totally tan, with platinum blonde hair. If it didn't fool whomever that idiot was, how could she possibly think about going back? She has to re-think her position about returning to her former life. She has a great new life. Why screw that up?

The hotel suite minibar held Mel's attention the rest of the night. She drank and she drank, and she drank some more.

At sunrise, Mel had figured out her next move. No one was going to decide her fate other than herself. New Mel was on to a new chapter in her life. After living all these years among the very rich, Mel knows she cannot give up this lifestyle and why should she? She loves her life. She loves the special attention she receives. Yeah, yeah, yeah, she made some mistakes along the way, but she's no axe murderer, she rationalizes.

Exactly eleven years and six months after exiting her former life, Mel emerges with her new face, fully transformed by a world-renowned plastic surgeon. The plastic surgeon altered her face in a way which positively changed her outlook on life. All traces of old Mel, including her self-image, were no longer. Old Mel had exited the planet forever. No one will recognize her with her shapely new nose, reduced chin, added dimples and cheek implants. The anxiety that once consumed her, is now gone.

Mel was patient with the healing process because she had no choice. She spent her days sipping ice cold champagne, listening to the classics, and exercising. She spent her nights sipping ice cold champagne, listening to the classics, and exercising.

Plastic surgery would create opportunities for her to continue growing in this new life. Although she faced years of sexual harassment by the same men she would later encounter as somewhat equals, she now understands how over sexualization works.

She decides to keep the platinum hair, but she had it re-shaped to give her an edgier look. The shorter, neater haircut made her look and feel different. Those unrealistic beauty standards are now the standard.

She also took an overnight flight to Tanzania and returns with beautiful, cloudy, gray eyes. A specialized plastic surgeon performed eye implant surgery a procedure which intricately inserts a beautiful gray lining into the space surrounding the iris. The addition of the eye color along with her fresh platinum blonde cut gives Mel the most exotic look she could ever imagine. Her reconstructed nose and the lip injections are the finishing touches.

Mel stands staring in the mirror at herself, trying to find traces of Old Mel. When she feels she is fully satisfied with her transformation, she is confident and now ready for her reentry into society.

Mel re-enters society, Cashmere Leigh. Her life as Cashmere Leigh would come from a totally different place. Cashmere will lead the life Mel always aspired to. Cashmere Leigh would lead the life Mel often daydreamed of. Cashmere Leigh had big plans. She planned to live!

Mel's new journey begins with the purchase of a downtown condo. This would not be your average condominium, as it is three full stories with a lighted lap pool and a separate private elevator. The elevator opens to Cashmere's living room. Her outdoor patio is heavenly, to say the least. At night, the stars appear to be within her reach.

With all her connections, Cashmere would soon be hobnobbing with the best of them, and before long, she had finagled her way into some slick social circles. Cashmere knew where the "in crowd" hung out and slowly infiltrated those circles, undetected. On a few occasions, she even ran into a few members of the executive crew from the Penthouse Suites. She begins attending all the functions of the upper echelon, hoping to develop friendships with the people who could usher her in. She is a lot more outgoing than her former self. Cashmere is very stylish, and her body image had greatly improved. The idea that no one recognizes her gives her another level of self-worth she had never felt before. She could live "that life" she always imagined.

Since her feet are now firmly planted inside the once closed door, she is focused on letting everyone know she has arrived. She immediately began seeking out organizations to volunteer her time and, of course, her money. Her social media pursuits revolve around the upscale classy events that brought in moneyed families with clout and status.

Cashmere began dining at the finest restaurants, establishing herself as a "big tipper" and making a habit of ordering dessert for fellow patrons. She would send over champagne service whenever she discovered a party was celebrating a milestone event. Hand-written notes wrapped around five crisp one hundred dollar bills were given to the top maître d's. She was sure to send notable floral arrangements and hefty monetary donations to the charities of the movers and shakers. These types of philanthropic organizations were known to reach out to their donors.

Soon, the word began spreading about the anonymous, generous socialite.

Cashmere was careful to take her time with all the service workers all over town. The extra care she took with them by generously tipping them paid off. Before long, the doors to the best places were always open to her.

Next, she began focusing on individuals. She starts a blog to entice those who ran in the circles she aspires to join. She read up on all the odd activities the rich, nouveau rich, and seemingly rich are involved. She makes every effort to show up for them. She signs the guest register at every charity polo match, luncheon, opening and groundbreaking ceremony that her money and style could get her into. She knows exactly what to wear for each occasion. Her wardrobe alone is enough to ensure entry into every affair. For every event she attends, she makes a mental note to follow up with a carefully handwritten thank you.

She does a happy hour tour around town, inviting her new followers to join her for "Drinks on Me!" This tactic creates a great following for her, and she reciprocates by tossing in hors d'oeuvres for her guests. Cashmere's fandom was blossoming, and she couldn't be happier.

Within a few months of her arrival, Cashmere's name was being tossed around for her graciousness, philanthropy, and her great get-togethers. Her efforts began paying off quite handsomely.

As she arrives home one evening, she finds a beautiful silver box waiting for her at the front desk. Inside is a personal invitation to attend a fundraiser for an up-and-coming political candidate.

The fundraiser turned out to be quite crowded. The candidate is well connected and there are many familiar faces among the invitees. The women in attendance are stunningly beautiful. Cashmere fits right in. A few times during the evening, she was mistaken for a Swedish model who was also in attendance. The very thought of being held to such a high standard of beauty was mind-blowing. Cashmere thought of herself as a good seven on her best days. Suddenly, she was a head turner with a bunch of suitors asking for her time. She enjoys the attention but is careful to elude the photographers who were all itching to take photos of all the guests. Maybe they weren't itching to get a photo of her, but it sure felt like it.

Cashmere mingled all evening, getting acquainted, building trust, making new friends, but mostly listening. She had to be careful not to speak too openly. Over the years, she'd become a powerful, trained speaker. She remembered to keep her speaking voice under wraps. She smiled politely and gave short statements when asked about the candidate.

The ultimate test would be an encounter with someone familiar with her. If she could engage someone from her past without detection, a new life was steps away. She had to be careful not to move too quickly.

She begins planning an intimate luncheon to support the local food bank. She overheard some of the guests at the last fundraiser mention the need to load up the food bank in the candidate's district. She immediately contacted the manager of the food bank and began planning. Since this would be her event, she would be in control of the function from start to finish. The planning that went into the fundraiser helped control the mini panic attacks she suffers, mostly due to her own self-doubts. The countless scenes she overplays in her mind—where she is finally captured and paraded, naked through the streets of the city, for everyone to point and ridicule is more than she can bear.

The "what ifs" were literally killing her. "What if someone recognized her" and "what if they were already onto her?" and "what if the event was not successful?" These questions began to swirl around her head the moment she began planning. Thank God she kept a hefty supply of champagne in the freezer.

To keep her anxiety at a manageable level, she hired an event planner she met through her social inner circles. "Nothing too gauche or over the top," she explained. Henri took copious notes, casually following Cashmere around her place. "It will be an intimate dinner for 40," she explains. "I want it done in all white, with beautiful white flowers all around the room. I'd like to have white scented candles that smell of jasmine, with white tablecloths and tiny votives lighting the tables. Every guest should have their place card written in calligraphy. Please order clear plastic chairs and have them draped with silk ties in the back, and I want the extra soft chair cushions, in white, of course. I want white orchids interspersed with white roses on the bar and at the entry."

"Got it, completely understated," Henri says. He closed his planner and set off to do Cashmere's bidding. Cashmere is quite pleased with her choices and can now breathe a sigh of relief, knowing Henri would make her vision come to life.

On the day of her big event, Cashmere spends half the day pampering herself. The special colorist she found dyed her tresses frostbite white. Her hair was laid beyond belief. The next stop was a visit with Ramon. Ramon was the best make-up artist in the city. He would give her a beat to remember. Ramon was a skillful artist. He meticulously transformed Cashmere into a fairy-like creature. He was beside himself when Cashmere left his salon.

The final step before the luncheon was a trip to Neiman's to pick up her perfectly fitted two-piece white, high-waisted silk suit. Cashmere stood at the entrance of her grand luncheon and greeted her guests. Among them were local artists, entrepreneurs, preservationists, and, of course, style and trendsetters. She was careful to invite and solicit those who were like-minded and civic-duty types. She invited the individuals who helped shape and preserve the city. She really wanted to set a standard for philanthropy. After living among those that led lives far beneath what would be considered the poverty line in this country, she felt compelled and empowered to do what she could to help the less fortunate. It made her feel good to be able to do something for others.

Having ill-gotten gains didn't bother her as much as the suffering of others did.

At the end of the luncheon, Cashmere and friends had raised over two hundred thousand dollars in donations from various organizations and individuals alike. Her newly formed LLC would make headlines the very next day. The caption in the society section read, "Leigh Foundation Raises Two Hundred Thousand Dollars in Donations for the Fourth Street Food Bank. Social media was trending about it as well. The Fourth Street Food Bank sent a shout out to Cashmere from the City Concert, which also contributes to the food bank."

Cashmere dined out every night following her successful event. Her plan had worked like a charm, but something was still missing. "Of course!" she blurted out loud, looking around to see who made the loud proclamation. Once she realizes it was her own voice she heard, she recognizes what she is feeling is loneliness. "Of course," she whispers this time, not wanting to draw attention to herself. What's missing is the camaraderie, the friendships, and most of all, the love of her sweet beau, John.

Cashmere was so caught up in her new life and being on the run and not wanting to be detected that she forgets about all she'd given up. Every now and then, she would allow herself to reminisce about the good old days, but her new life is far more exciting to even think about giving it up. Then there's always that pesky little thing called "jail" that really keeps her from going there with her thoughts.

The nagging void in her life would linger a few days more and consume her thoughts. For whatever reason, she somehow can't get past the hallmarks of her old life. These thoughts would inevitably bring her to the crossroads. Will she be able to go on as Cashmere Leigh, giving her new life purpose and continue to build on that life, or forever pine over a life now lost?

Determined to come to grips with a new life, Cashmere snaps out of this funk and begins planning her next event. She enjoyed how her philanthropic efforts made her feel, and she would use that feeling as the catalyst to restart the fire simmering inside her. Her next charitable event would be solely dedicated to the public-school systems in underrepresented districts. She could feel the adrenaline rush coming on as she began to forge ideas on how this gala would play out.

One day, while out purchasing door prizes, Cashmere happened upon the sweetest cafe she had ever laid eyes on. Once inside, she was instantly drawn by the ambience and the smell of the most intoxicating aroma of coffee. The cafe is decorated with oversized velvet couches in various shades of purple. There were lavender loveseats in the back of the cafe. The ceiling was completely covered in beautiful crystals that twinkled like colorful stars. Cashmere was awestruck by the mood of the cafe. It brought her back to her days with John. She found herself seated in a lush, deep purple couch before long. The young waitress brought over the wonderful concoction for her to sample. She quickly asks for a full cup and slowly drinks in the entire atmosphere.

She falls into a dreamlike video world of her own, mixed with times from the past and present. The most intriguing part of this daydream is the vivid picture of Cashmere living her life with a man who seems to adore her. She knows that allowing herself to daydream in this way only produces an overwhelming sadness that takes her days to overcome. This was a continuing sign of a life lived unfulfilled. Sometimes, her daydreams would allow Cashmere to live a free, open existence. This was her chance to simply be.

Cashmere's vision is interrupted by the cafe's owner, Palmer. "Would you like another cup of heaven?" Palmer asks with a bright smile that lights up the room.

Coming out of her reverie, Cashmere responds, "You bet I would? What's in this coffee?" she asks.

"Well, if I tell you, I'll have to kill you," Palmer jokes.

Cashmere would go on to spend hours at the cafe joking with Palmer, listening intensely to the details of Palmer's life. She learns that Palmer, along with her father, are the owners of the cafe. The ladies are instantly connected and chatted the afternoon away. After a while, Cashmere heads home, armed with Palmer's contact information and the promise to return. Cashmere hopes the two of them could become friends, real friends—in a very real sense.

Cashmere's growing status among her social media followers and among her fellow philanthropists was growing. People were drawn to her low-key demeanor, quiet sophistication, and, of course, her beauty. She had begun to realize how to balance herself over time, and the combined traits were winning people over. In the midst of preparing for her gala, Cashmere did forge a friendship with Palmer. The two women are a stunning pair to look at. Their exotic looks, which were in complete contrast to each other, turned heads wherever they went.

Cashmere, the ethereal-looking beauty from the Nordic regions, and Palmer, the dark-haired, blue-eyed Princess from the East, are quite the pair.

With the two of them hitting the restaurants and attending social gatherings together, their impeccable taste in clothes, and the inexplicable aura surrounding them, the duo become the sweethearts of the social scene. The invitations start pouring in for them.

Cashmere is careful to accept invitations in a controlled atmosphere. For her purposes, that means dark settings, limited exposure to the paparazzi and first-hand knowledge of who would be in attendance. It was one thing for the paparazzi to catch glimpses of her and Palmer, gallivanting around town. She's always partially disguised with tasteful dark sunglasses, hats, caps, scarves, or a combination of all of them. Even though her new look doesn't resemble old Mel, she's still careful not to press her luck.

Cashmere's life, from the outside looking in, is everything any woman could want. Everything except for love. Not only does she not have a special person in her life, but she feels she cannot trust anyone with her secret. Even in the confines of her home, she dares not to whisper anything that resembles her former life. No one and nothing that resembles her past can ever see daylight. Cashmere would find other ways to fill the void that love brings. Living vicariously would become her new jam. Love must be avoided at all costs.

While preparing for her big event, she realizes she had forgotten to invite Palmer's father.

She had heard many great stories about him from Palmer, and she felt like she already knew him. Cashmere immediately sent an additional ticket to the gala for Lawson to attend.

The gala was completely sold out, and there was a significant buzz in the air. The night had finally arrived. Cashmere was both amazed and annoyed with the amount of attention her event created. She was sure her gala would not receive the kind of attention she was getting as the guest list would include mostly teachers, administrators, social workers, and the more bookish types. She also invited those who would give generously to the cause, but she didn't think an event of this type would garner so much attention.

All in all, the fundraiser was a huge success, and the proceeds were split between several public schools in need of bathroom remodels, laptops and iPads, and a much-improved school breakfast and lunch programs.

During her travels, Cashmere saw the importance of education and how educating every child gives them more opportunities to become successful and useful citizens. She saw what education did for her colleagues in the corporate world and wanted those same opportunities for all children. This event brought pure joy to Cashmere. This time, her LLC would be sending out six-figure checks to the schools that so desperately need these funds.

On occasion, Cashmere finds herself tearing up at the thought of her accomplishments. Besides the unexpected turn out and sizable donations to her favorite recipients, she receives the unexpected admiration from a man in attendance. The admiration is coming from a very unexpected place, and Cashmere is not amused. The man just happens to be Lawson Ferguson, Palmer's father.

Lawson Ferguson, in name alone, comes with a standard of class and sophistication.

Not the type of manufactured class and sophistication that Cashmere created, but the kind of class and sophistication that he genuinely owns. For those reasons, Cashmere takes on an instant disdain for Palmer. She reads him from the beginning and automatically dislikes everything about him. From her perspective, Lawson Ferguson is educated in the old-fashioned, stately way. She imagines he is quite a moralist, full of arrogance and self-righteous nobility.

Cashmere never mentions her dislike for her father to Palmer. Palmer would be simply crushed to know how Cashmere feels about her favorite person on earth. Lawson reminds Cashmere of all the men who believe their ideas, education, point of view, styles and the air they breathe is better than that of a mere woman. She decides Lawson's style, behavior, personality, and vision are quite the contrary to her own. She becomes obsessed with how much she dislikes him starting with his overpriced, overrated ugly shoes, obviously garish but expensive socks, custom trousers that reek of tailor made, fitted silk shirts with diamond encrusted cuff links, and last but certainly not least, his awful, paid too much for, wool and silk blended suit coats. She imagines he's just like the arrogant, high octane, overtly confident, Ivy leaguers she has grown to abhor. Lawson Ferguson reminds her of the men who placed a glass ceiling on her career. Because of all the things she so very confidently believes he represents; she decides she wants no part of him.

From day one of sizing up the competition Mel realizes she is just as smart and just as talented as many of her colleagues, but every year, she is passed over for consideration as an officer of the company. She was never even offered the position of junior executive. A man with less abilities and talents would surely become an executive within any corporation. Pretending to not care about the disappointment became more and more heart wrenching, each year. Making the decision to stay and re-dedicate herself to winning and finding ways to live up to the expectations kept her eye of the prize. Congratulating her fellow colleagues on their promotions without gagging was her greatest challenge there. Secretly burying her middle finger during the congratulatory handshake always made her feel a little better.

Anyway, Lawson Ferguson wouldn't get anything more than a hello from Cashmere, if that.

Cashmere would spend days at the cafe, carving out strategies for her next event. She loves spending time at the cafe, even though "he" was always lurking around from time to time. In spare moments when he wasn't looking in her direction, Cashmere glowered at Lawson, figuring he was a silent partner to Palmer. She decides Lawson's ideas were probably being hypnotically injected into practice and her dear friend, Palmer, had no idea. Palmer was way too kind and gracious to know when she was being used.

On occasion, Cashmere would catch a glimpse of Lawson staring in her direction. She would return the glimpse with a stare that would undoubtedly lead to his death. Lawson, on the other hand, was drawn into Cashmere's silvery gaze. He would try to engage in mutual eye contact with her, only to be left staring at the back of her head or receiving a steely, cold look of disgust.

Lawson thinks it's amusing that Cashmere despises him so much. He imagines she was once hurt by someone she truly cared about. Lawson decided to play it safe and keep his distance. He likes her, but enough to get his gonads kicked in.

The two of them always play nice in Palmer's presence, whom they both adore, but quickly retreat to mutual corners when Palmer is out of sight. Lawson's unrequited admiration for Cashmere would remain unchanged.

Many months passed and the distance between Lawson and Cashmere had grown ever so. The day came when Lawson announced his return to his home in the Coral Sea Islands. Lawson was known as the Unofficial Mayor of the Islands as there were few inhabitants living there. Lawson lives abundantly among the forested islands. There, he built a home for he and his cherished wife. The home was a beacon among the backdrop of lush green gardens, shimmering waterfalls, and stunning native plant life. When the house was completed, Lawson rushed back to New York to finalize his business closings and finally capture the life of leisure he so desired. He collected a cool $eight hundred seventy million dollars after cashing out his stock options, selling off his real estate holdings, and liquidating everything that Palmer didn't want for herself. Lawson allowed himself to daydream the life he would never have…

At long last, Lawson and Faun Ferguson would be free to spend their lives among the breezy, most breathtaking autumnal foliage in the world. Lawson commissioned an architect, skilled in the preservation of protected wildlife, to build a small castle surrounded by the unmatched natural beauty of sea coral reefs. The sea creatures of varying sizes and colors would swim and dance about the castle walls and floors through heavy glass panels. Lawson had the home built with the intention of never having to leave home. There was nothing left to the imagination that wasn't thought of. The house is both magical and logical. Its beauty is incomparable.

The idea of Lawson going away is a subject that piqued Cashmere's curiosity. Through her friendship with Palmer, Cashmere would learn that Lawson spent years agonizing over the sudden death of his wife, Faun, Palmer's mother.

It was during Palmer's graduate year in college that the family learned of Faun's tragic death. Faun and a gathering of her closest pals were out for the evening when an out of control 18-wheeler plunged through the glass pane window of the restaurant where they were seated, killing Lawson's wife and her friends instantly.

When the land where the cafe stood became available for purchase, Lawson and Palmer leaped at the chance to make it their own. The pair leaned heavily on each other through the tragedy and worked tirelessly to make a go of the cafe. Faun loved that restaurant so much that both Lawson and Palmer knew that they had to have it. They would preserve Faun's memory through Cafe Faun.

Cashmere is moved by the loyalty and love shown by Lawson toward his wife. The announcement that he would be leaving to "go home" hit her differently than she ever imagined. She spent so much time hating him for her perceived image of him and now he is leaving. She suddenly felt vulnerable to him and sadness for his loss. Cashmere has firsthand knowledge of what loneliness and fear feels like. Still, there was another emotion nagging at Cashmere toward Palmer. She couldn't quite figure out what the emotion was, but she was pretty sure she still hated him. Or maybe she just hated what he stood for. Yeah, that's it, she hated what he stood for. Oh yeah, and his clothes. She hated his Brooks Brothers clothes.

Lawson's days in the states were clicking down on the calendar, so Cashmere invites him to accompany her to dinner one night. Cashmere makes it crystal clear that it is a mercy date to allow Palmer the opportunity to run the café without his interference. Palmer is making strides in running the cafe without Lawson's careful supervision, so she asked Cashmere to keep her father busy so she could guide the ship, alone, for a change. Palmer also wants her father to live his life. She knew he would never leave her if he didn't feel confident, she would be okay. Café Faun saved both Palmer and Lawson's lives. The café gave them something to look forward to, to dream of and to find joy in again.

Cashmere would do all that she could for Palmer. If it means being nice to her old man and dragging him around town, she will stifle her eye rolls and fake smile her way through the times with him. She begins by asking Lawson to accompany her to the events she and Palmer are scheduled to attend. Cashmere and Lawson begin going to the gym together, to the movies, running errands, and picking up supplies for the restaurant. Their daily jaunt to the flower mart to hand select fresh flowers became their favorite errand. Cashmere loves the smell of fresh flowers and spends a great deal of time schooling Lawson on the biology of plants. Lawson never heard one word regarding the flowers as he is drawn in by Cashmere's fragrant perfume and flawless eye for detail with her wardrobe. Palmer is so grateful to her friend for this huge inconvenience and promises to make it up to her when Lawson is gone.

During a visit to the cafe to take Palmer out for a much-needed escape, there is a small kitchen fire that delays their getaway. Cashmere parks inside her favorite booth, checking emails and returning calls. Suddenly and unexpectedly, Lawson slides into her booth and, without hesitation, professes his love for her. All those times, seeing her at the cafe gave him a shift in mindset that he thought was impossible. His love for Faun could never be replaced, but he had grown very fond of Cashmere over time. He confesses his repressed feelings for her and hopes she feels the same.

The dead silence that followed could be interpreted in so many ways. Lawson is uneasy as he rethinks his position. He wonders if this is the beginning of the deadly silent treatment women love to use as a weapon against lowly underserving men? He's more than certain she's alive as she blinks periodically.

Cashmere is dumbstruck. Her sudden connection to this man is a scary feeling. She had already realized his outlook on life, his values, his loyalty, and his overall decency as a human being was everything she could want from her man. She understands him, and she believes he understands her. Her struggle to be happy is as great as his. But the question is, could he just love her without judging? Could she share her innermost feelings with this man? Could he or would he forgive her for what she's done? Could he truly love her heart? For the first time in her life as Cashmere Leigh, she could only cry. She cries with a sadness that comes from a deep wound within. Here she comes face to-face with the love of her life, but she cannot have him. Lawson is indeed a good man, a very good man. He deserves so much better than her.

Lawson sits holding Cashmere for hours on end. Palmer closes the cafe and heads home. Lawson promises to call his daughter later. Palmer leaves the cafe in tears, not knowing why her friend is so distraught. Cashmere simply could not face Palmer. She cries even harder when Palmer turns out the cafe lights, leaving her limp in Lawson's arms.

By the end of the night, Cashmere had shared the stories of her life with Lawson. She tells him of her life in corporate

America, her whirlwind life as a millionaire lottery winner, her travels abroad and the many people she met along the way. She speaks in detail about what she has done and how she came to be. Lawson could only stare at Cashmere as the stories and horrors of her life unfold.

Lawson is silenced by the physiological condition of the woman before him. Cashmere's body shakes uncontrollably at times, then suddenly lays limp from complete exhaustion and embarrassment.

The sudden focus on her was suffocating as well. She knows Lawson's image of her is completely shattered. She is certain he will go home to his island castle and forget she ever existed.

This ability to say all these things out loud is painful and emotional for Cashmere, but she is finally able to say what she had done. She no longer considers the consequences of what could happen to her going forward, nor does she care anymore. She is finally free of all the pain she's caused, the lies she's told, the awkwardness, the cover-ups, the exposure, the guilt, and most of all-her regrets.

Conclusion

It was a cold, rainy day in January when Lawson Ferguson set sail for his beloved Coral Island home. There, he would live in the place he was so very emotionally attached to. He has such a physical love for his home, and the passage of time away only strengthened his longing. Lawson could feel his heart breaking at the thought of leaving his daughter, Palmer, behind. Lawson and Palmer spent the holidays together and had such a good time that it was very hard leaving her. Although he believes he is leaving her at a time where she is mentally and physically capable of running the business on her own, he would prefer she could be with him instead. He is, however, so very proud of Palmer's accomplishments and dedication in making the business as successful as it has become. The restaurant is now her passion, and that passion has changed her life.

She would be moving into her first home within weeks and was "totally jazzed" her words, with idea of decorating from scratch. Palmer and Lawson made a pinkie promise to get together soon. They also promised to face time each other every weekend.

Palmer waved goodbye to the departing cruise ship until it became a speck in the vast ocean. The rainy season was upon them, so it wasn't apparent to either of them that they were both crying through their smiles.

Both Palmer and Lawson realized there would be moments of grief and uncertainty, but they must get on with their lives. Their dependency on each other was borne of grief and protection in coping with their loss. This prolonged grieving nurtured their relationship and enabled them to support each other and weather the worst storm of their lives.

The emotions were beginning to well up in Lawson's throat as he headed back to his cabin. Many of the passengers on the luxury cruise line had already departed for their cabins. This wasn't the typical cruise ship, full of fun and merriment. Severe weather conditions were expected this time of year. The weather was cloudy and dark, and the rain was coming down steadily. Lawson stands motionless, allowing the rain to echo all around him. His return to his home is bittersweet, but a must.

As Lawson steps inside the cabin, Cashmere hops into his arms and begins showering him with kisses. Lawson's mood is instantly lifted. He drinks in the affection of his beautiful bride. Mr. and Mrs. Lawson Ferguson tied the knot on New Year's Day. Palmer was their flower girl and maid of owner. The three of them spent every single moment they could together before the happy couple set sail.

Life was just beginning for the Fergusons as they sail into their new world.

The End